the Collector

the Collector

K. R. Alexander

Scholastic Inc.

All rights reserved. Published by Scholastic Inc., *Publishers since 1920.* SCHOLASTIC and associated logos are trademarks and/or registered trademarks of Scholastic Inc.

The publisher does not have any control over and does not assume any responsibility for author or third-party websites or their content.

No part of this publication may be reproduced, stored in a retrieval system, or transmitted in any form or by any means, electronic, mechanical, photocopying, recording, or otherwise, without written permission of the publisher. For information regarding permission, write to Scholastic Inc., Attention: Permissions Department, 557 Broadway, New York, NY 10012.

This book is a work of fiction. Names, characters, places, and incidents are either the product of the author's imagination or are used fictitiously, and any resemblance to actual persons, living or dead, business establishments, events, or locales is entirely coincidental.

ISBN 978-1-338-21224-2

10 9 8 7 6 5 4 3 2 1   18 19 20 21 22

Printed in the U.S.A.   40
First printing 2018

The text type was set in Sabon.
Book design by Nina Goffi

For those who want
to know what goes
bump in the night

6

This was *not* how I wanted summer vacation to end: driving with my mom and my sister through cornfields on our way to my grandmother's house. Not for a fun weekend visit, but for good.

I was ready to be bored.

I was ready to be lonely.

But I wasn't ready to face off against an evil power that wanted me dead.

1

"Do I get my own room?" Anna asked when we drove down Grandma Jeannie's driveway. "Josie snores."

I glared at her from the front seat. Sometimes my little sister could be such a pain.

"Yes, Anna," Mom said. "You both get your own rooms. It's an upgrade, see?"

"You need internet to get upgrades," I muttered, crossing my arms. Grandma Jeannie didn't have any internet service. My phone barely even worked out here.

"Josie . . ." Mom began, but she didn't finish her

warning. She'd already told me many times not to make a fuss, because this was hard on everyone.

Yeah. Sure.

She didn't have to start sixth grade at a new school in the middle of nowhere.

Grandma's house came into view. It was huge—much bigger than our apartment in Chicago had been. This place had three whole stories, with big windows on each side and a porch that wrapped all the way around. A big yard stretched out on all sides, and past the swing set and small apple orchard was a thick forest that looked like it was filled with brambles and secrets. Even now, on a warm evening, the trees looked dark and cold.

The front door opened and Grandma Jeannie came out. She was shaky and leaned heavily on the screen door, but she was smiling. Even though I really didn't want to be here, seeing her made me smile, too. It was rare to see her smile like she actually saw us.

"Oh, my girls!" she called when we got out of the car. She took a shaky step toward us. "I'm so happy you made it!"

Mom jogged up the steps to hug Grandma while Anna and I got our bags from the back of the car. There weren't many—Mom had shipped a few boxes ahead of us, and the rest of our life was in storage.

"Hi, Grandma Jeannie!" Anna said, running up to hug her. I was right behind.

"Oh, my girls," Grandma said again. I looked at Mom; her smile looked forced as she watched Grandma. But then Grandma looked back to Mom. "How was the drive, dear?"

"It was fine, Mom. I think we're all a bit tired, though."

"Well then, I have some sun tea in the kitchen. Why don't we have a drink out here before dinner?"

Mom agreed and went inside to get the tea while Grandma led Anna and me to the patio table.

She's an old woman, Mom had reminded us a million times on the ride there. *Her memory's fading, and she might not always make sense. Just be patient with her and act like you know what she's talking about even if you don't. That way she won't get too flustered.*

"Now, girls," Grandma Jeannie told us once we

were settled, her voice a strong whisper. "There are three rules for living here. One, never leave your windows open after dark, even if it's hot. Two, no dolls in the house. And three, never, ever go by the house in the woods. That's where Beryl lives."

She looked out to the forest when she said it. I stared, too. It gave me a chill. Anything could be hiding out there. Whenever we'd visited before, she'd never let us out of her sight. But she'd never mentioned a house before. Or Beryl.

Who or what was Beryl?

I wanted to ask, but I didn't want to upset her. It was clear from her eyes that it upset her enough just to say the name.

"Don't worry, Grandma," I assured her, patting her arm. "We'll follow the rules."

Mom came out then and handed us the sun tea. I didn't really want it—I wanted soda—but Grandma Jeannie didn't have that, so I needed to get used to it now.

Grandma and Mom talked about the drive for a bit. I tuned them out. I was trying to prepare myself for tomorrow, my first day at a new school in a new town. It made my stomach hurt to think about it. How was I going to find my way around? How would I make friends? What if the kids made fun of me because I wasn't from around here? I'd already stopped worrying about what Grandma had said— her rules were strange, but that was just how things were here. The only thing I could do was follow along.

I only tuned back in when Grandma started talking about Grandpa Tom.

"He'll be right down, you know," Grandma said. "He'll be so happy to know you're here."

Mom went quiet. Anna shot me a shocked *Can you believe she said that?* look.

Grandpa Tom had passed away five years ago. I barely remembered him.

"Let's get you inside, Mom," our mother said. "I think maybe you could use a nap."

"Tom will be so happy," Grandma continued. She let Mom help her up and guide her toward the house.

"Girls, could you get the rest of the bags?" Mom asked. I knew she just wanted us to keep busy. She hated seeing Grandma like this.

It seemed to be happening more and more often. That was one reason we were here, to make sure Grandma wasn't in danger. Mom was worried she'd fall down the stairs or hurt herself. And when Mom lost her job, it made sense for us to come here. Or at least it made sense to the adults. It still didn't make sense to me.

All we knew was that Grandma wasn't entirely with us anymore. Some days she was better than others.

And we also knew not to go into the woods.

As soon as Anna and I were a safe distance away, heading to the car while Mom led Grandma inside, Anna asked, "Do you think she's okay?"

I shrugged.

"That was weird about Grandpa, right?"

I shrugged again, wishing she'd get the hint that I didn't want to talk about it.

But she went on. "Who do you think Beryl is?"

"You ask too many questions," I replied. I started lugging the suitcases from the trunk while she grabbed another bag from the back seat.

A breeze blew from the woods, and I heard a noise

that sent another wave of chills down my back. I stopped what I was doing and looked into the trees. Nothing moved.

"What are you looking at?" Anna asked. I nearly jumped out of my skin.

"Did you hear that?" I asked her.

"What?"

I looked away from the woods, back to her.

"Nothing," I said. "Come on, let's get these inside."

I didn't want to be out there any longer.

That noise . . .

I swore I'd heard an old woman laughing.

2

"Josie?"

Anna's voice was quiet. But since it came unexpectedly at me through the darkness of my room, it nearly made me scream.

I was in bed, staring at the moon out the window and still worrying about what tomorrow would be like. She was supposed to be asleep. We had school in the morning.

"What do you want?" I grumbled. I sat up and looked at her—she was peering through the crack in my doorway. I could see her stuffed bear dangling from her hand.

She didn't answer at first. Instead, she looked back, as if she was worried that Mom was going to catch her. Then she stepped into the room and closed the door quietly behind her.

"I was wondering if I could sleep in here?" she asked.

I groaned. My first night with a big room all to myself, and Anna was having nightmares again.

"Anna, we already talked about your bad dreams."

She shook her head before I finished my sentence, then crept up to my bed.

"It's not dreams," she said. "I haven't even fallen asleep yet."

Another groan from me. We'd had *that* talk, too, how sometimes when you dream you don't think you're dreaming, but it still isn't real. Anna had a hard time distinguishing reality from dreams. Mom said I was just like her at that age, but I didn't believe it.

"You're seven years old," I said. "You're too big for bad dreams."

"I wasn't dreaming!" she yelled. Then she slapped

a hand to her mouth while I shushed her. *"Sorry,"* she whispered. "I said I wasn't dreaming. I heard something. From the woods."

That made me sit up straighter.

Part of the reason I was still up was from thinking about school. But another part, a part I didn't want to admit, was that I couldn't stop hearing things from outside. *Coyotes*, I told myself. *Or owls.* I'd watched enough nature documentaries to know that a lot of animals woke up at night to hunt, especially in the forest. The noises were natural. Even if they were scary.

"They're just animals," I said.

"Animals don't laugh," she whispered back.

"Some hyenas do." I knew there weren't hyenas in Illinois. But she didn't need to know that.

"They weren't animals," she replied. "I know it. I think they were talking about us."

I shivered.

"Are you sure you weren't asleep?" I asked.

She shook her head again, her stuffed bear hugged tight. "Positive."

"Fiiiiiiine." I rolled over and pulled back the covers for her. "But this is the last time. I still haven't forgiven you for telling Mom I snore."

"But you do," Anna whispered. "You're like a train."

I couldn't help it—I giggled. She could be so serious sometimes.

Anna giggled, too, and curled over.

"Goodnight, Josie," she said.

"Goodnight, Anna. Don't let the bedbugs bite."

"They won't bite me—they'll be too busy nibbling on you!"

I giggled again, but I didn't fall asleep right away.

I lay there for a while, listening as her breathing slowed down and occasionally snuffled—if anyone snored, it was her. I couldn't get what she'd said out of my head. *I think they were talking about us*. I knew it was stupid to believe her. She'd probably fallen asleep without knowing it and had slipped into a strange dream.

But that didn't make me feel much better. *I'd* been hearing something all day, too.

Something from the woods.

Something from the one place we weren't supposed to go. And if it was calling to Anna, too, that meant it was real.

And it wanted us.

3

I knew it was a bad dream.

I knew it was a bad dream because I wouldn't have walked into the woods on my own at night.

Still . . . I could smell the sharp tang of crushed berries and sap, could hear the snap of branches under my feet and the howl of distant wind. I could feel the biting cold on my skin. I could taste the fear in my throat as I walked.

I didn't know why I was dreaming of the woods behind Grandma Jeannie's house. I didn't know why I wasn't waking up. I just knew I had to keep walking. If I stopped walking, *she* would find me.

If she found me, I was dead.

The woods were dark but the moon above was full, so I could see the faint path at my feet. Maybe I should go a different way. But no, if I did that, I'd get lost, and then she'd definitely find me, and I would definitely be dead. I had to keep moving. Had to stay warm.

I had to find . . . something.

But what?

Keep walking. Keep walking.

Something snapped behind me. A branch? A bone? I turned around. My heart was beating so loud and fast I could hear it. A shadow moved between the trees. The flash of teeth. Of glowing white eyes.

I ran.

I ran, and she ran after me.

I could hear her now, crashing through the trees. Calling out. Calling my name.

"Josieee. Josieee."

She was getting closer. I ran faster. Branches tore at my legs and hit my face, but I didn't stop. She was so close. I could hear her breath. I could smell her breath. I could *feel* her breath, burning the back of my neck.

There.

Up ahead.

Through the trees.

There was a light. A window. A house.

Grandma Jeannie's—it had to be. She would keep me safe. Grandma Jeannie always kept us safe.

I ran harder, and the creature behind me was howling now, howling and laughing. Like a wolf. Or a hyena.

Or an old woman.

I was so close to the light. To home.

But when I burst through the trees, I knew I was wrong.

It wasn't Grandma Jeannie's house.

It was old and the paint was peeling. The yard was overgrown and filled with broken statues.

I didn't have time to care. I ran up the path to the front porch. The lights were on. Someone had to be home.

I pounded on the front door.

"Please!" I yelled. "Please let me in! She's coming for me! Please, help!"

A shadow moved behind the curtain.

The creature howled behind me.

The door opened.

I looked at the person who opened it . . . and it wasn't a person at all.

It was a doll. A doll the same height as me, with blank eyes and a sad smile.

"Welcome home, Josie," she said.

Before I could scream, before I could run, the doll's cold fingers wrapped around my wrist, and she yanked me inside.

4

"You look like you didn't sleep well," my mom said at breakfast.

I shook my head and poured myself some more orange juice.

"Annie slept in my bed," I said, casting a glare at my little sister. "She hogged the covers."

"Only because you snored!" she replied.

Mom looked at the two of us. She was clearly confused.

"Why didn't you sleep in your own room?" she asked.

"I heard—"

"She was being a baby," I interrupted. I didn't want Anna telling Mom about the voices from the woods. Mom was stressed out enough already. She didn't need anything else on her mind. "She was having bad dreams."

"I didn't!"

But Mom clearly believed me. She walked over and gave Anna a hug. "Oh, honey. Everyone gets bad dreams. Especially when they're staying in a new place."

I didn't want to tell her I was having bad dreams, too. Neither of them needed to know.

"Where's Grandma?" I asked instead. I didn't want to talk about dreams anymore.

"She's out back. She likes having her breakfast outside."

"Can I have my breakfast outside?" I asked.

She didn't answer right away.

"I guess, sweetie. Just don't bother your grandma."

"I won't," I promised, and picked up my cereal and juice and walked to the back deck.

Grandma Jeannie was sitting on a rocking chair when I opened the back door. She didn't look at me when I sat down on the chair beside her. I knew the chair used to be Grandpa Tom's.

For a while we both sat out there, eating and watching the birds fly around the backyard. The air was already warm and sweet, and when I looked at the woods, I couldn't figure out why I'd been so scared of them yesterday, or why they'd given me nightmares. They were pretty. Sure, there might be wild animals in there, but that wasn't scary. That was nature.

"Today's my first day of school," I said. I looked at Grandma. "Did you ever go to school here?"

She didn't answer at first. I wondered if maybe today was going to be one of her "bad" days.

Finally she said, "I grew up in this house." She took a sip of her tea. "And I went to the same school that you are." When she looked at me and smiled, it looked a little sad. It sort of reminded me of the creepy doll from my dream—sad, and trapped. "You're following in my footsteps."

"Did Mom go to school here?" I asked even though I already knew the answer.

"No, Josie. We sent your mother to a private school over in Joliet. We thought it would be better for her."

It was the same answer Mom had given me.

"If it's better, why don't I go there?"

"Because it's too late to register you." Grandma Jeannie reached over and patted my arm. "Don't worry. It's a good school. You'll make plenty of friends."

I didn't want to talk back, but I couldn't help rolling my eyes. Right—the school wasn't good enough for my mom, but it would be good enough for Anna and me. This was going to be *great*. I wondered if all my "new friends" would be the imaginary kind.

"I just want you to promise me one thing," Grandma said.

"What?"

"Whatever you do, don't go into the woods."

It was so strange for her to mention the woods when we were talking about school, I almost laughed. But Grandma sounded very serious, so I didn't.

"I know the rules, Grandma," I assured her.

"Of course you do. But I'm your grandmother. It's my job to keep you safe."

"What's so dangerous about the woods, anyway? They're beautiful. We went to the parks in Chicago all the time."

I knew I shouldn't say it. It was as close to talking back as I'd ever come with my grandma. But I really wasn't looking forward to school, and I was upset enough that I couldn't hold back.

"Beauty can hide great evil," Grandma Jeannie said. "The woods are deep, and Beryl is hungry."

"What's Beryl? Is she a bear?"

"Beryl is a woman," Grandma said gravely. "And if she has her way, all of us will be dead."

I wanted to know more. But Mom opened the door at that moment and told me it was time to go to school. I hugged Grandma good-bye.

She whispered in my ear.

"Remember."

5

By lunchtime I had decided that my new school was horrible, and I was going to move back to Chicago tonight whether Mom wanted to or not. I'd call a taxi. I'd get a plane ticket.

There was no way I would stay in this school.

Even though it was only the first day of class, everyone already had their friend groups, and none of them would let me in. It was like I was wearing a huge sign that said NEW CITY GIRL—kids giggled whenever I said my name or answered a question. (I stopped answering questions after second-period math class.) A couple stopped and whispered to each other when I walked by in the halls—what had they heard about me? Others crashed into me, as if they wanted to see how I'd react. I don't think I'd ever felt my face blush so much in my life.

Running into the woods behind Grandma Jeannie's sounded like a much better time than this.

The cafeteria was its own kind of forest. There I was, at lunch, sitting at the end of a table all by myself. I didn't know what I'd been served. Some sort of meat loaf covered in brown gunk. Mashed potatoes that were clearly from a box. Frostbitten peas. A brownie that was as hard as a rock and probably tasted like a rock, too.

I didn't eat meat. It made me wish I was back at my old school—at least there we could get the salad bar. I imagined if I asked the lunch staff here for a salad, they'd give me a plate of grass.

Tears formed in my eyes as I pushed the food around on my plate. I was hungry, and I was homesick, and I hated it here. Back home I'd be eating lunch with my best friends—they were doing it right now. We'd laugh about our science teacher, or talk about which kids we thought were cute. Then we'd plan to hang out later, after school. I missed them. All of them. I couldn't even call or text because I couldn't get reception anywhere in this backward town.

I *hated* this place.

"Can I sit here?" a girl's voice above me asked.

I didn't look up. It was probably someone just playing another joke, and I didn't want to be the punch line again.

"Excuse me?"

That made me look. I'd been bumped into a dozen times in the hall, and no one had said excuse me. Especially not with that accent. She didn't sound like she was from around here. Like me.

For a moment, I thought maybe she was imaginary. She was *definitely* not from around here—she was in really nice jeans and a simple black top, and she had a ton of bracelets on her arms and perfectly manicured nails. She also wore a vintage locket on a gold chain around her neck. Her hair was long and curly, and when she smiled she had huge dimples. And she was wearing makeup. But unlike anyone else here, she knew how to put it on.

She looked familiar somehow. But maybe that was because she looked like someone I'd see in Chicago, not someone I'd see here.

"Hi?" I asked.

She laughed. "Why was that a question?"

"Because I don't know why you're talking to me." I looked around at the rest of the cafeteria. "Everyone here pretends I don't exist. Unless they're making fun of me."

The girl looked around the lunchroom.

"Don't worry about them. They're simple."

She said *simple* like it was a curse word, and it made me suddenly grateful she didn't think that *I* was simple.

She set down her lunch box and held out her hand.

"I'm Vanessa."

"Josie," I said, taking her hand. She had a very firm shake, and her fingers were cold.

"May I sit?"

I didn't realize she was still waiting for my permission. I nodded.

"Thank you," she replied. She sat down, but she

didn't start eating. "So," she said, looking at me intently. "You're new here?"

"Yeah. My sister and I moved in with my grandma yesterday. I'm from Chicago."

"Why would you leave Chicago for this?"

I almost answered with the truth—Mom lost her job, and Grandma was losing her memories—but then I remembered this Vanessa girl wasn't one of my old friends. I barely knew her.

"Mom wanted a change from the city," I said. I hoped that made us sound sophisticated, not lost.

"Definitely a big change," Vanessa said. "Well, don't worry, Josie. I'll take care of you."

I didn't know how to respond to that. So instead I pushed around the meat loaf a bit more.

"My first job as your friend is to tell you not to eat that," Vanessa went on. "I think it's the same loaf they served last year."

I told her I was vegetarian, and she said she thought she was the only one in the whole town. Or had been, until I came along. I don't know why that made me feel better, but it did. At least I felt a little less alone.

She started telling me about which teachers were good and which were bad, and which kids I needed to avoid—which was pretty much everyone. The way she described the place, it seemed like she was the only one here who might understand me. And, looking around, I believed it. The kids who watched us stared openly. I felt like a zoo animal. I turned my attention back to Vanessa—having her there made me feel a lot less singled out.

I listened intently. I was so caught up in what she said I didn't even notice that I'd eaten most of my peas and managed not to break my teeth on the brownie.

By the time the lunch bell rang, I still hated it here . . . but I hated it a little bit less than before.

Vanessa was a lifesaver.

She walked me to my next class after lunch. Somehow, just having her around made my life easier; no one bumped into me in the halls and no one called me any names. In fact, it almost seemed like people stepped out of the way when we passed. If they seemed to be paying me any attention, it was more out of shock than anything else.

I knew what they were thinking:

How did the new girl become friends with the coolest girl in school?

I honestly didn't know how either. But I wasn't about to question it, not when she seemed like the only thing that kept me from getting shoved into a locker "on accident."

A few periods later, I stepped into my English classroom—nervous as always—and there was Vanessa. I'd spent the day having to find a seat beside people who clearly didn't want me around, based on the snickers or the pieces of paper that got thrown at me. This time, though, Vanessa smiled like she'd been waiting for me. She moved her books from the desk beside her so I could sit there.

Had it really been that easy? Had I really just made such a good friend?

All through that class, no one giggled and no one threw anything at me. Not even when I raised my hand to answer a question.

Vanessa was even waiting for me after school. While the rest of the kids ran off to catch a bus or get a ride home, she stood outside by the flagpole. Once again, she smiled when she saw me.

Before I could walk over to her, Anna stepped

beside me. The school was so small they had all the grade levels in one building.

"How was your first day of third grade?" I asked her. We started walking toward Vanessa.

"I hate it," she replied.

"Oh no, why?"

She didn't seem to want to answer at first. Instead, she reached into her backpack and pulled out her little teddy bear.

"Kids were mean to me," she said. She sounded like she wanted to cry.

"They were mean to me, too," I replied. "But look! I made a friend."

"I'm Vanessa," Vanessa said, shaking Anna's hand. "You must be Anna. Josie told me so much about you!"

I couldn't remember saying anything to her about Anna, but that wasn't surprising—we'd talked about a lot at lunch, and I'd probably mentioned Anna at some point. Besides, Anna was smiling so hard at being noticed I didn't want to question it.

"How was your first day?" Vanessa asked.

"Kids were mean to me," Anna replied. She took my hand as she said it. "I want to go home."

Vanessa looked concerned, but then her smile returned.

"You don't want to go home! It's only the first day. I'm sure you'll make a new friend soon."

"Everyone hates me," Anna replied.

"Oh, don't say that. I'm sure there are some great people you haven't met yet. You just have to give it time!"

Vanessa reached into her purse and pulled out a piece of candy.

"I'm not supposed to take candy from strangers," Anna said diligently. I could tell she really wanted to take it. She'd always had a sweet tooth.

"I'm not a stranger—I'm Josie's new friend. Which means we'll be friends, too. Even after you make one of your own."

Anna smiled and took the candy. Vanessa handed me a piece.

"Do you want to come over to our house?" Anna asked.

"That's so polite of you," Vanessa said. It made

me wish I'd asked first. I was going to, but it seemed awkward, especially since it was only our second day with Grandma Jeannie. I was partly relieved when Vanessa said next, "I'm afraid I have to go home and take care of my aunt. Maybe next time. I just wanted to make sure Josie got through the day okay."

"I did," I told her. "Thanks."

Vanessa smiled like I'd given her the biggest compliment.

"Good. See you at lunch tomorrow! It was a pleasure meeting you, Anna."

Vanessa turned and walked away. I wondered if her aunt was going to come pick her up or if she would walk home. The school was in the middle of nowhere, and town seemed like a very long way to walk—if that was where she actually lived. I hadn't gotten around to asking her.

"She's really cool," Anna said, watching Vanessa go. "You're lucky. I wish I had a friend like her."

"You will," I said. I pointed to the parking lot, before she could start getting sad. "But look, there's Mom!"

Anna did a little jump and let go of my hand to run over to Mom's car.

I felt the little bubble of happiness inside of me deflate. Meeting Vanessa had made my day, but now I remembered I had to go back to a house with no TV and no internet and barely any cell phone reception.

It made me wish Vanessa had accepted Anna's offer to come over.

Though I was still a little worried that Grandma Jeannie would only manage to scare her away.

7

"What was that?"

Anna's voice shook when she looked up from her toys. We were playing by the old swing set in the backyard. Well, *she* was playing. I was up in the small fort, working on my math homework. Why did teachers think it was okay to give us homework on the first day?

"What was what?" I asked. I didn't want to climb down and see. I was too full from the spaghetti Mom had cooked to move.

"That noise."

"I don't—"

She yelped, and before I could finish the sentence she was scrambling up the ladder. She nearly crushed my homework when she came up.

"Careful!" I yelled, but she shushed me immediately and pointed one shaking hand toward the woods.

I went quiet.

For a while, I didn't hear anything except my heart and Anna's quick breathing. A few minutes passed. I was just about to tell her to go back down and keep playing, because she was being silly, and I had to finish my homework before it got dark.

Then something rustled in the woods.

My skin got goose bumps, even though it was warm and the sun was still shining above the trees.

"What—" I whispered. Another rustle cut me off.

Because it wasn't just the sound of something creeping around and snapping bushes.

I heard a voice.

An old woman's voice.

"*Joooosieeeeeee,*" it hissed. Like wind in a graveyard.

Like the voice that chased me in my nightmare.

"You can hear that?" I asked Anna.

She nodded solemnly.

I didn't even bother grabbing all my homework. I took Anna by the hand and bolted.

8

I didn't get mad at Anna when she asked to sleep in my room that night. Honestly, if she hadn't asked first, I might have asked her. I didn't want to be alone in the too-big room, with its too-big windows over-looking the too-dark forest. It felt like the shadows could attack me in there. Even with the night-light on. (I had to ask Anna to bring hers in, because I was supposed to be too old to sleep with a night-light.)

I'd had to ask Mom to bring in my homework ear-lier. There was no way I was going outside again. I made up some excuse about feeling dizzy when I climbed the ladder. I didn't think she believed me, but she still owed me for moving us out here, so she went and got it. When she returned, I studied her reaction to figure out if she'd heard anything. It didn't look like she had. Had I just been imagining things? Maybe I was letting Anna's overactive imagination influence my own.

Even with the night-light and the closed windows and Anna beside me, I didn't get much sleep. And not because Anna was hogging the covers.

Every time I closed my eyes, I remembered my nightmare. Being chased through the woods, and the creature calling out my name.

"Josie?" Anna whispered. Her voice caught me off guard—I'd thought she was asleep.

"Yes, Anna?" I whispered back.

"Do you think she's after us?"

"Who?"

"Beryl."

I shivered again. I still had no idea who Beryl was, or why we should be afraid of her. Or why Anna would think the mysterious woman Grandma warned us about was the voice we heard in the woods. Though I couldn't think what else it could be.

"You know what Mom told us about Grandma Jeannie," I said. I tried to keep my voice down, but I also tried to keep it strong. I had to convince myself, too. "Sometimes she doesn't remember things right. Like who or where she is. I bet this is part of that."

"Do you really think so?"

"I do."

I didn't.

I went on. "Whatever we heard was just our imagination. The wind or something."

Anna went quiet for a few moments.

"I dreamed about it last night," she said. "That I was being chased. Through the woods."

I shivered. "Did you find an old house?"

I shouldn't have asked it. I didn't want her to know I'd had a similar dream.

"Yes," she said. Her voice was even more scared now. "But I woke up before I went inside."

I couldn't stop—I had to know.

"Did you find a doll?"

She didn't answer. At first, I thought she had fallen back asleep. I tried to relax and closed my eyes. Then, right when I started to feel myself go heavy, she whispered:

"The doll found me."

9

If Anna had another nightmare, she didn't mention it when she woke up the next morning. She seemed to be perfectly rested, even though she'd spent the whole night tossing and turning and keeping me awake.

I couldn't stop yawning at breakfast.

"Couldn't sleep again?" Mom asked.

I shook my head. She knew that Anna had slept in my bedroom, but I didn't want her to think Anna was the reason I'd been up all night. Otherwise Mom might force Anna to sleep in her own room, and that seemed worse than missing sleep. I wished Mom would let me drink coffee. At least in emergencies like this.

Before she could ask me any more questions, I excused myself from the table and went out to sit with Grandma Jeannie on the porch. I had orange juice. I'd heard vitamin C helped give you energy.

"Grandma?" I asked.

"Yes, dear?" she replied. She was at the edge of the porch, watching the trees with a serious look on her face. She didn't look away.

Feeders hung from the eaves of the porch, and hummingbirds were dancing about. It was beautiful and calm, but I couldn't stare at the woods without feeling scared.

"Who's Beryl?"

Just like that, Grandma's attention snapped back. She looked at me.

"Who told you that name?" she asked. She no longer sounded like my grandma. She sounded angry. And mean.

"Y-you did."

Her eyes narrowed and I worried she was going to start yelling— something that I'd only seen happen

once, when Mom was trying to convince her Grandpa
Tom wasn't coming back from the store.

Then she brought a hand to her forehead like she
had a headache.

"I . . . I did . . ."

"Grandma—"

"You must stay out of the woods!"

"I know, Grandma. I am. But who is Beryl?"

"*Never* say her name!"

"But who—"

"*She's after you.*" Grandma brought down her
hand. She sounded very tired, but very serious. "I've
heard her, in the woods. You must never go in there.
You must promise me you'll never go in there. I can't
protect you there, but I can protect you here. If she
ever catches you, she'll gobble you up."

"Mother." My mom opened the porch door and
stepped out. "What are you two talking about?"

"You should never have brought them here,"
Grandma Jeannie said, turning to Mom. "It's not
safe. It's not safe."

My mom came over and put a hand on Grandma's
shoulder.

"What are you talking about, Mom?"

"Must tell Tom," Grandma Jeannie said. "Beryl is awake. Beryl is coming. Tom . . . Tom will know what to do."

A hurt expression crossed my mom's face. She studied Grandma for a moment, then me.

"Go get ready for school, Josie," Mom said firmly.

I opened my mouth. I wanted to ask more questions. I wanted to know who Beryl was, and why my grandma thought she needed to keep us safe. But I knew Mom's look—the time for questions was over. I'd have to ask Grandma tonight.

I looked out to the woods before heading back inside to pack my bag.

It felt like I was being watched.

10

I could barely stay awake through my classes. Even with Grandma Jeannie's strange warning ringing in my ears, making me scared of the trees outside the school window, I kept yawning. I didn't raise my hand for any questions. I couldn't even follow along when we were reading aloud. Which turned out to be okay, because the more I kept my head down, the less people seemed to stare at me. It was like they'd forgotten I'd existed, or else me being new wasn't so interesting anymore.

Vanessa was waiting for me at lunch, though she didn't seem to have a tray. I set down my tray of gross food—some frost-burnt, old lasagna—beside her. I still hadn't figured out how to eat vegetarian here. Maybe once my mom settled in, I'd ask her to pack me a lunch. Until then, I was going to have to make do with a bag of chips that, according to the numbers at the bottom, had expired last month.

How was the lunch here even legal?

"I wouldn't eat any of that," Vanessa warned when I sat down.

"How do you survive?" I asked.

She smiled and pulled out her lunch box.

Inside, there were two of everything: two sandwiches, two bags of chips, two bananas. And four chocolate chip cookies.

"I asked my aunt to pack extra," Vanessa explained. She paused when handing me the sandwich. "That's okay, right? I don't mean to be rude by assuming."

I didn't know what made me feel warmer—the fact that she thought of bringing me food or the fact that she was worried it might hurt my feelings.

"No. Thank you so much."

I felt myself blushing. I didn't think anyone would

do anything that nice for me ever again. Something about the new town made me feel like nice things just didn't happen here. Except Vanessa. She was the only good thing in this place.

Vanessa smiled and began eating her own sandwich. It was cheese and a bunch of vegetables. And the cookies were definitely homemade.

"My aunt likes making food for people," she said. "And she was so happy to hear I'd made a new friend. I heard her talking on the phone to one of her friends . . . she was worried I was never going to make friends here."

"But you seem so cool. Like you own the school."

She shrugged and took a bite of her cookie.

"I'm not popular. People are just intimidated by me, so they leave me alone. You're the first person who feels like an equal. Like we could really be friends."

Her smile came back.

"I'm glad you moved here, Josie. It's been lonely."

I couldn't tell her I was glad I'd moved, too, because that would be lying, and I knew better than to do that.

"Where are you from?" I asked instead, because I realized she knew everything about me and I knew nothing about her. She was the one who had asked all the questions yesterday.

It was definitely the wrong thing to ask. Her smile disappeared, and I immediately felt bad. She didn't answer.

Instead she changed the subject and started talking about the English homework from yesterday, and how it was totally unfair that some of the teachers were already doing quizzes. I agreed. When she asked me questions about Anna or my grandma, I answered like I didn't feel weird that she'd ignored my own question.

I yawned a couple times. On the fourth, she giggled.

"Am I that boring?"

"No, I'm sorry. I didn't sleep much."

"Bad dreams?"

I shook my head.

"No. My sister slept in my room. She's scared of the woods."

Vanessa looked at me for a bit. I couldn't tell what she was trying to discover.

"There's nothing to be scared of in the woods," she said. Her voice sounded different. Flat. Like she was reciting a line from a story she'd read, but didn't believe. "It's just trees and animals."

"She's probably just scared because it's a new place," I said.

Vanessa nodded. Then she asked me more questions about Chicago and what my friends were like and what I did for fun. I tried asking her a few more things, but she never answered them. Maybe she just didn't like talking about herself. A couple of my friends back home were like that, too. Especially the ones whose parents were getting divorced or who had other problems. I didn't want to push it—if Vanessa stopped talking to me, life would be horrible.

Without her, the school would be just as scary as the woods.

11

At the end of the day I found a note folded up inside my locker.

STAY AWAY FROM VANESSA GRAVES

There was no signature. I looked around, wondering if maybe someone was playing a prank. But no one was paying me any attention. I crumpled up the note.

Someone was just jealous that I was friends with the coolest girl in school. And I wasn't going to let them scare me away from her.

12

Anna was waiting for me on the school steps when I walked out. And, much to my surprise, she was smiling.

"Did you have a good day?" I asked.

Anna nodded.

"I made a new friend," she said.

"That's great!"

"Yeah. Her name is Clara. She's new here, like us." She lowered her voice and looked around. "People make fun of her, too. We want to start a club together."

I smiled and hugged her. Anna sometimes didn't get along with other kids her age; this was really good news. It also meant I didn't need to feel guilty that I'd already made a friend. Even though someone was trying very hard to keep Vanessa and me from being friends.

"Is she here?" I asked.

"No, she took the bus."

Vanessa came over then.

"Hi!" she said.

I felt bad because when I saw her I got knots in my stomach. Even though I'd thrown out the note, I felt like maybe she would be able to tell. Like she could read my mind and knew what I'd seen.

Someone was just being mean. Trying to keep me friendless and unhappy. Or maybe they thought it was a threat—maybe Vanessa had an admirer who didn't want her to have other friends. Though that was silly, since it didn't seem like Vanessa talked to anyone besides me.

What did the note mean? Was I supposed to be scared of Vanessa or scared of someone else?

When Vanessa hugged Anna, my fears disappeared completely. Anyone who was nice to my sister was a good person.

"What are you doing tonight?" I asked Vanessa.

"Gotta take care of my aunt again," she said with a frown. "She loves cooking, but she needs help around the kitchen. She just had knee surgery."

"Oh," I said. "I thought maybe you could come over."

"I can't really leave her right now," Vanessa said. "Maybe you two could come over tomorrow night?"

I was surprised she was inviting my sister, too. And a little upset. Anna had her own friend now. First my bedroom, and now my friend? I needed to figure out some boundaries with Anna before she took over my life here.

"Yeah!" Anna said. "Can I, please?"

"We'll have to ask Mom," I said. "But hopefully we can."

I couldn't imagine Mom would let us go over to a stranger's house. Still, weirder things had happened.

Vanessa smiled huge. "That would be awesome! I'll make a big dinner. And I have internet!"

That sold it. I'd told her at lunch that we didn't have internet at all, and I couldn't really contact my friends at home because the service was so bad. Suddenly, the note in the locker was long forgotten. Vanessa was, once again, a lifesaver. What had I done to be so lucky? I couldn't imagine how miserable I'd be in this tiny town without her, and I'd only known her a couple days. She was just that sort of person—the moment we met, we were destined to be best friends forever.

Mom drove up a little later and waved to us.

"Do you want a ride?" I asked again.

"No, thanks," Vanessa replied. "I like the walk."

She came up to the car with us, though, and introduced herself to my mom. Mom offered to drive her, and Vanessa politely refused again.

"Can we go to Vanessa's tomorrow?" Anna immediately asked. "She has internet!"

I could tell my mom was tired—I wondered if Grandma had been in a bad state all day.

"Of course, if it's okay with her parents."

"I'll ask my aunt," Vanessa said. Vanessa seemed to emphasize the word *aunt*, which made me wonder . . . where were her parents? Why did I not know that yet? "I'm sure it will be okay."

We said our good-byes, and Vanessa stood and waved while we drove off.

"She seems nice," Mom said.

"She is," I replied.

"I made a new friend, too!" Anna called from the back seat. She proceeded to tell us all about her new friend, Clara. I was still a little upset that she was going to Vanessa's with me, but it was okay. She'd become better friends with Clara, and then she'd be out of my hair for good.

13

Grandma was on the back porch when we got home.

Mom watched her sadly out the back window, like she wanted to go and talk to her or bring her inside. But Anna needed help with her homework, so Mom was distracted from whatever it was she wanted to do or say.

I went out and stood by Grandma's side.

She had perched herself at the railing. She was muttering under her breath, and she didn't look away from the woods when I approached.

I hovered there for a little bit. I couldn't understand what she was saying.

It sounded like a foreign language, and her fingers twitched in weird patterns.

"Grandma—" I whispered.

She didn't stop speaking the strange language. It felt like I'd rubbed a balloon over my arms—I tingled with static electricity.

After a while, she made some complicated hand gesture. Then she sighed and slumped against the railing. She looked older than I'd ever seen her.

"That should keep her away for a while," Grandma Jeannie said to herself.

"Who?" I asked.

I knew who.

"Beryl," Grandma said. She looked at me. There were tears in her eyes, and that scared me more than the woods or the note. "She knows about you, Josie. She knows about you, and she wants to take you away."

14

Grandma didn't say anything else at dinner. She acted normal, and Mom was more than ready to pretend that we were all one big happy family. The funny thing was, it sort of worked. We sat around and ate takeout Chinese food (I didn't know where it came from—I hadn't seen any restaurants in town), and Anna didn't talk about missing Chicago once. In fact, she couldn't stop talking about her new best friend, and all the fun they had at recess and their secret codes and the club they wanted to create where only the coolest kids could join. She said I could be a member if I swore a secret oath . . . once she figured out what the oath was going to be.

I finished my homework, and Anna read an old book of Grandma Jeannie's. When it was time to go to bed, I almost thought I would once more have the room to myself.

Then Anna snuck in.

"Can I sleep in here?" she asked.

"Are you hearing things again?" I asked in return. I put away my book and pulled back the covers for her before she answered.

She hurried over and snuggled in. I was starting to wonder if I'd ever actually get my own room. Maybe she would invite her new friend over some night and they'd build sofa forts or something, and then I could have some peace and quiet.

"No," she said when she was comfortable. "I'm not hearing anything. But I'm scared I might."

I nodded. I hadn't heard anything either. The woods were awfully quiet tonight. I wondered if maybe Grandma Jeannie had been doing a spell earlier to keep us safe.

Just the thought gave me goose bumps and made

me feel silly at the same time. Grandma Jeannie couldn't do spells. She wasn't a witch. She was just an old lady with Alzheimer's.

It didn't seem to matter, though. A few minutes later, Anna fell asleep. I lay there and watched the shadows on the wall and kept my ears peeled, hoping to hear something in the woods. Well, maybe not hoping. I don't know what I thought.

If I heard something, it meant there was a creature out there.

But if I didn't, it meant one of two things: Either there never had been a creature in the first place, or Grandma Jeannie was a witch . . . and the monster chasing us was real.

15

I could barely wait for the school day to be over. Every class seemed to drag on, and we even had a pop quiz in math. After what seemed like forever, the final bell rang, and I met Vanessa on the front steps of the school along with Anna.

"Are you two ready?" Vanessa asked with a smile. "It's kind of a long walk."

"We'll be fine," I replied.

My fingers itched to map the destination on my phone, but I'd left it back at home—there didn't seem to be service anywhere near the school and it just drained my battery. I could only hope we would get a ride from her place back home. I wasn't very good with directions or getting to places on my own, and I didn't know how we'd get back to my place. Grandma Jeannie lived far away from the main town.

I'd tried to get more information about what we were doing when Vanessa and I chatted at lunch, but she only wanted to talk about me. Like always. She'd asked me all about Chicago and my friends there and what I liked to do in my free time. Probably just because she wanted to know what she should plan for tonight. It's not like the town provided many options.

Even though I was excited to be heading to Vanessa's house, I still felt a little nervous. It was silly. But I swore that kids were watching us walk away together like they were scared. Not of me or Vanessa, but *for* me.

There'd been another note in my locker.

VANESA IS DANGERRUS.

It had been in a different handwriting. And the kid who'd written it clearly didn't know how to spell.

All it meant was that a group of mean kids were trying to scare me away from my only friend. Well, Vanessa was being nice to me and everyone else in the school acted like I had a foot growing out of my head, so I didn't care what they thought.

Vanessa took Anna's hand and started skipping down the road. I felt silly for a moment, but then I jogged up to them and skipped alongside. Within a few seconds, I was laughing, the school and its mean kids forgotten.

The trees rose up around us, smelling fresh and green. The sun was warm and the breeze was sweet. We skipped along the main road for a bit, and then took a path off the sidewalk that cut through the woods.

Anna's hand immediately tightened in mine.

"What is it?" Vanessa asked. She slowed down and looked at Anna.

I didn't expect my sister to tell the truth. She did.

"I'm scared of the woods." Then she looked at me. "We both are. Grandma Jeannie says we're not supposed to go in there."

I felt my cheeks blush hot.

"It's okay," Vanessa said. She gave Anna a big smile. "The woods are only scary because they're new to you. I know where we're going. You're completely safe with me around." Then she winked at me, and I felt my blush go even deeper. I didn't want her thinking I was scared of the woods, too.

I was, though.

We continued on. It was probably just my imagination that made the light get heavier and the noises quieter, but after a while it felt like we were somewhere entirely different. I couldn't explain it: The trees were the same and it wasn't like it was suddenly midnight. It just felt like we were in a different forest in a different time. A time when fairy tales were real and big bad wolves roamed the woods.

I could understand why Grandma thought this place was dangerous.

We'd stopped skipping a while ago. I still held Anna's hand.

Vanessa walked in front of us, her feet dancing lightly on the path as she led us deeper and deeper.

"How are we going to get home?" Anna whispered. Her voice was so quiet I barely heard her.

"Don't worry," Vanessa said, somehow hearing Anna. She looked back. I hoped it was my imagination, because in here, even her face and smile looked different. Sinister. It must have been the light. "I'll get you both home. My aunt can't drive right now, so I'll walk you back."

More goose bumps. I didn't want to walk through the woods later. But I didn't think we really had a choice—either we kept going, or I made a fool of myself and lost the only friend I'd made.

"Thanks!" I said. I tried to be cheery. It was probably too much. "That would be great."

Vanessa just smiled again and led us farther into the woods. I tried not to look through the trees. I tried not to imagine what or where Beryl was, prowling about like a wolf on the hunt.

At least I hadn't had any more nightmares. Last

night I'd dreamed I was at a pizza-eating contest with my friends. Not scary at all.

Finally, when my feet were hurting and it felt like we'd been walking for hours, the small path opened up into a gravel road.

"Just a little farther," Vanessa said.

Seeing the road made me feel a bit better—at least there was a way for cars to get here. Particularly police cars and ambulances.

We rounded the corner and saw her house. I stopped dead in my tracks.

It was the house from my nightmare.

Vanessa walked a few more steps before realizing that Anna and I had stopped.

"What's wrong?" she asked.

What *wasn't* wrong? There were broken bird-baths and mannequins in the front yard, surrounded by a fence that was mostly moss and collapsed wood. The roof was covered in mossy shingles; a tiny tree grew up from the gutter. About the only thing that made the house look lived in were the intact windows and the light glowing from inside.

"Nothing's wrong," I said, way too late for it to be convincing.

Concern crossed Vanessa's face. When I realized why, I felt terrible.

"I know," she said. "It's not really nice to look at. My aunt hasn't been able to work because of her knee, and my uncle died a few years ago. I'm really the only one keeping the house running." She bit her lip and looked sad, kicked a rock at her feet. "I completely understand if you don't want to hang out here. I can walk you home now." Her voice wavered a bit. I wondered how many potential friends she'd taken here, only to get rejected.

Maybe that's why kids told me to stay away from her—they probably thought she was a bad person because she lived in a house like this.

I wasn't about to let their meanness get in the way, nor was I going to let Vanessa feel bad about her house. That wasn't what was important.

What was important was that I'd seen it in my nightmare, but there was no way I'd be able to explain that. She'd think I was crazy.

"No, please," I said. "I don't want to go home yet. I just . . . well, it's very . . . *unique*. I was surprised."

Vanessa perked up a little bit. But there were still tears in the corner of her eyes.

"That's a good word for it. I'll be the first to admit the place is a bit weird. Especially on the inside. My aunt is quite a collector."

This was the last possible point that Anna and I could have turned back.

But when Vanessa said, "Come on" . . . we went.

16

Vanessa hadn't been lying about one thing: Her aunt was definitely a collector of strange objects.

Getting closer, I saw that besides the old mannequins and broken-down baby carriages (complete with baby dolls with spiders living in their eyes), the birdbaths had piles of doll heads covered in moss. I tried not to look too closely as Vanessa led us up her overgrown path toward the house, but it was impossible not to stare. The whole place smelled like wet earth and leaves, and it was definitely colder . . . but maybe it was just because the trees leaned in here, making the whole place shaded and eerily quiet.

I kept trying to tell myself that I hadn't actually seen this place in my dreams. It was some weird déjà vu or something.

Then Anna stopped and whispered in my ear, "I don't want to go in there."

"It's okay," I replied. "She's our friend. It's just a strange house and we don't want to be rude."

Anna seemed like she wanted to argue, but she didn't get the chance.

Vanessa unlocked the front door and opened it, and rather than a creepy life-size doll staring out there was just the scent of cinnamon and baking cookies. The hallway inside looked warm and bright and completely normal. Just like any other house. Anna clung to my arm tightly in spite of how welcoming the place looked.

For a moment, I was reminded of "Hansel and Gretel"—this place didn't look like a gingerbread house built by a witch, but it sure smelled like cookies meant to lure in small children.

"Come on in!" Vanessa said. "But please take your shoes off at the door."

I couldn't imagine an evil witch asking kids to

take off their shoes. My imagination was just running full speed. Vanessa was just a girl and this was just a quirky house.

We went in and took off our shoes. Vanessa closed the door behind us. I got a small bit of relief from noting that she didn't lock it, but that relief was short-lived. Because next I noticed the dolls.

They were everywhere.

Dolls the size of my hand and dolls as big as me. Every shape and color and size, wearing every type of clothing you could imagine. There were dolls in dresses and dolls in overalls, dolls with long hair or short hair or no hair at all.

Hundreds and hundreds of dolls.

I couldn't see their faces, though. Because every doll was facing the wall.

Every. Single. One.

Anna wouldn't budge from the doorway. I didn't move either. I could see into the rooms just off the hall, and they were filled with dolls, too.

"Oh," Vanessa said, noticing our hesitation. She had been heading down the hall like it was the most normal place in the world. But when she stopped to look back, she fingered her locket and bit her lip. "Yeah. I guess I should have mentioned those."

She walked up to a doll and touched its head. She almost looked a little sad.

"My aunt's been collecting these ever since she was a little girl. She has too many to count." She laughed slightly. "I tried getting her to sell them a few times, but she loves them like they're her children. Dusting is a nightmare. They . . . they take some getting used to."

"I guess you *did* say she was a collector."

"You have no idea," she replied.

"Why are they looking away?" Anna asked. Her voice was a whimper.

"That was my doing," Vanessa said. She giggled a little. "I moved in a few years ago, and they really creeped me out. I asked her to hide them, but she said she liked having them on display. But she said I could turn them around so they weren't always looking at me. So many eyes . . . ." She shivered theatrically and then smiled. "Come on. I think my aunt made cookies! And there aren't nearly as many dolls in the kitchen."

Reluctantly, Anna and I followed her in.

It was almost worse walking down the hall and having all the dolls facing away. Like they were scared or ashamed or in time-out. I kept waiting for one to turn around and glare at us. Anna clutched my arm so tight I hoped she didn't leave a bruise. She was probably wishing she hadn't come along. Even with the promise of internet.

At least the kitchen wasn't as cluttered with dolls. There were a few on a spice rack, and one sitting inside a hanging saucepan, and a couple on the fridge (which was covered in old doll-shaped magnets). Compared to the hallway and the rooms I'd glanced at in between, the kitchen looked pretty normal. The appliances were fairly new and the counters were cleared. No clutter. In fact, save for the dolls, everything in the house seemed to be pretty organized. I guess, in their own way, the dolls were organized, too.

And, as the smell promised, a plate of chocolate chip cookies was laid out on the kitchen table.

"Would you like milk with your cookies?" Vanessa asked.

She ducked into the fridge as she spoke—the inside was also fully stocked. Okay, minus the dolls, I guessed the place wasn't that strange. Maybe it wasn't so bad. I'd had a friend in elementary school whose parents collected lawn flamingos, inside and out. I told myself this was about as weird. Nothing to be worried about.

"Yes, please," Anna said. She seemed to have already forgotten about the dolls—she had a cookie in hand and was sitting at the kitchen table, eating away happily.

I asked for a glass as well and sat next to Anna.

"Where's your aunt?" I asked.

Vanessa paused for a moment.

"She must be asleep." Her eyes glanced at a closed door off the kitchen as she poured us milk. "Her new medication tires her out. I bet she got exhausted after making us cookies. I told her you were coming over."

I immediately felt guilty that her aunt had made herself tired just so we could have cookies. Even though they were a little burnt, I didn't say anything. I ate three. I didn't want her aunt to feel worse if she came back to a full plate.

We sat around and talked for a while. Vanessa asked Anna all about her classes and teachers, the friends she was making, and what she thought of the school and the town. I was used to Anna being quiet around people—strangers and my friends, especially—but she was so talkative with Vanessa that it almost felt like listening to a different person. Anna even started telling Vanessa things she hadn't told me yet, like the names of the kids who were mean to her and which teachers she thought smelled bad.

"Do you like living with your grandmother?" Vanessa asked.

"She makes us follow these weird rules," Anna said. She didn't even lower her voice. "Like we can't leave the windows open at night. But that's okay. There are bad things out in the woods. That's one of the rules, too. We can't go in the woods." She looked outside. "I guess we broke that rule, though."

"Anna," I said warningly. I glared at her; she was too far away to kick under the table. Though it was too late now.

"It's okay," Vanessa said. "Everyone has different rules. And your grandma is right—the woods *can* be dangerous if you go out alone. But there haven't been any bears or anything like that for . . . well, forever, I think. I've never seen any."

"It's not bears," Anna said despite my warning glares. "It's monsters."

That made Vanessa laugh. I looked at her, suddenly wondering if she was making fun of us or thought we were stupid, but it didn't seem like it. If anything, she seemed to take my sister seriously.

"What sort of monsters?" Vanessa asked, all smiles gone.

"I don't know," Anna said. "But I hear them at night. They give me bad dreams. One time, I dreamed about—"

Crash!

Anna and Vanessa both jumped. I pretended to as well.

What they didn't know was that I'd intentionally pushed my glass of milk off the table. It had shattered on the floor, spilling milk everywhere.

I felt bad for breaking a glass and making a mess. But I would have felt much, much worse if Anna had given our dreams away. Vanessa was my friend, so it should have meant I could trust her with anything. But my dreams were a line I didn't want to cross with anyone.

"I'm so sorry!" I said as I hopped off my stool. "It was an accident."

"It's okay!" Vanessa replied. She went and got some paper towels and a broom. I helped her clean it up, being very careful not to get cut on the glass. "It happens all the time."

When she went to the back porch to throw the glass in a trash can, I went over and whispered into Anna's ear.

"Don't you dare tell her about our dreams!"

"Why not?" she asked, clearly confused and a little hurt. "She's our friend."

"Yes. But that doesn't mean you should tell her everything."

"Why—"

Vanessa came back in then, and I shot Anna another glare before going back to mopping up the spilled milk. Hopefully she would listen. If not, she *definitely* wasn't staying in my room again.

"Would you like another glass?" Vanessa asked.

"No," I replied. "That's okay. We should probably get going. Mom wanted us back for dinner."

That was another small lie. Mom wanted us back before dark, but that wouldn't be for a few more hours. I just didn't want to wait around on the chance that Anna would say something I'd regret. Next time, I was going to be coming here without her.

"Aww," Anna whined. "I haven't even gotten to use the internet!"

"Next time," I replied. I tried to smile warmly at Vanessa. It was hard; I knew if I dragged this out, Anna would *really* start protesting. "We don't want to wear out our welcome."

It was something I'd heard my mom say many times, when she wanted to leave but didn't want to be impolite.

"You aren't," Vanessa said. She sighed, and for some reason that made her look sadder than she should have been. "I don't get friends over very often."

It made me feel really bad for her. Being unique also often meant being lonely.

"I'll definitely be back over," I assured her. I was very careful not to say *we* so Anna wouldn't say I was lying later. "Our mom just gets a little nervous when we're in new places, so I don't want her freaking out now."

Which was true. Back in Chicago, it had taken her a good month to be comfortable with me staying over at my friends' places for more than an hour. And that was *after* she got to meet their parents. I wondered if Vanessa's aunt would be well enough to meet my mom soon. This place was creepy, but it was at least a little better than inviting her over to mine.

I didn't want to have to introduce her to my grandmother—after Anna's blabbing, I was almost embarrassed.

"Before you go . . ." Vanessa said. She didn't complete her thought, just skipped out of the room.

"I don't want to go yet," Anna said, frowning at me.

"I'm your older sister," I replied. "And I say it's time to go home."

She opened her mouth to argue, but Vanessa was back then. She had something hidden behind her back.

"This is for you, Anna," Vanessa said. "I've had it since I was your age."

She revealed the hidden gift. My heart dropped when I saw it.

It was a tiny porcelain doll, old and wearing a faded sun dress. It was very creepy—and there was no way Grandma Jeannie would allow it in the house.

"I don't think I can," Anna said, looking at me for reassurance.

"It's okay," Vanessa said. "You can give her back in a few weeks if you'd like. She's a very special doll— she keeps bad dreams away."

I was torn. I knew that we couldn't bring the doll back—it was against Grandma Jeannie's very strange rules. But I also knew that it would be rude to decline, and that having the doll would mean Anna wouldn't want to stay in my room anymore. It would be nice to sleep on my own. I couldn't remember the last time I'd had real privacy. And maybe, if I could get over the embarrassment, it meant the potential to have Vanessa over for slumber parties.

Anna didn't answer. She kept looking at me for guidance.

"That's a really nice gift," I said. I went over and took the doll, examining it. It was even creepier up close—one of its painted eyes was smudged, and its smile looked . . . well, evil. One corner was twisted up, almost in a sneer.

If it helped Anna sleep, though, it was worth it.

"I think it's very nice of Vanessa to let you borrow it," I said, handing it to Anna.

"But Grandma—"

"Grandma Jeannie will understand. She doesn't want you having nightmares either."

I thought of her standing on the porch yesterday afternoon, muttering what I thought must have been a spell or gibberish. It seemed like Grandma Jeannie was trying very hard to keep us from having nightmares.

But that was just silly. Grandma wasn't a witch, and the doll wasn't magic—it was just something to convince Anna that she wasn't having bad dreams, even though it wasn't actually doing anything.

"Thank you," Anna said. She took the doll and hugged it close.

"Okay, we better go. It's probably a long walk back."

Vanessa shook her head and smiled, then pointed to the woods we could see through the backyard.

"It's not a long walk at all. Your grandmother's house is right through there. We're neighbors."

It felt like my heart stopped and everything went cold.

We weren't just in the woods.

We were in the woods behind Grandma Jeannie's house.

We were where Beryl lived.

17

When my heart starting beating again, it was hammering like a drum.

"What did you say your aunt's name was again?" I asked.

"Oh, I didn't. Her name is Tilda Morgenstern. I call her Auntie T."

I sighed in relief. It wasn't Beryl. We were safe.

Vanessa didn't notice my reaction—she was already at the front door, putting her shoes on. Anna cast me a wide-eyed gaze. She also knew we weren't supposed to be here. These woods were dangerous. And Anna had a doll. Two strikes against us.

"There's a shortcut between our houses," Vanessa said. "It goes right through the woods—we can be there in five minutes."

"No!" I said a little too loudly. I looked at Anna. "Sorry. I mean, I think we'd rather take the long way." I tried to think fast. "My mom said it was tick season."

Vanessa smiled.

"City people," she said. But unlike when the kids at school said it, she didn't sound rude. I could tell she was just joking. "Okay then, the long way it is. I'll walk with you. I don't want you getting lost." She made spooky hand gestures. "The woods can be a scary place."

Then she giggled and patted Anna on the shoulder. I tried to chuckle, too, but I couldn't. A part of me felt silly for being scared of the woods and believing Grandma Jeannie. Another part of me felt I should be taking this more seriously.

I decided that taking Grandma Jeannie seriously would mean losing Vanessa as a friend, and right now I needed a friend more than I needed to follow Grandma's rules.

Anna and I were going to have a lot of secrets to keep.

It took about twenty minutes for us to get back home. Once we left the grove where Vanessa lived, the path opened up and was sunny again. It was easy to forget that we were apparently in dangerous territory. Or at least in territory my grandmother thought was dangerous. Now that it was daylight, I couldn't figure out why I'd allowed myself to be scared of these woods. It was just trees and birds and sunshine.

Maybe I wouldn't follow Grandma Jeannie's rules too closely. Especially if we were going to be living with her for a long time.

I did make sure that Anna hid the doll in her backpack the moment we got to the main path. I didn't want to risk Grandma Jeannie's anger, and who knew if Mom would be driving past? It wouldn't surprise me if Mom was driving around looking for us—or, as she would put it, "keeping an eye out."

We didn't see her, though, and Vanessa dropped us off just before the winding drive leading to Grandma's house.

"Do you want to come in?" Anna asked.

"No, thanks," Vanessa replied warmly. "I need to get back and make dinner for my aunt. I'll see you at school tomorrow! And sweet dreams tonight, Anna."

She winked at me in a way that seemed to say, *Hopefully now you'll get a full night's sleep.* I hoped so, too.

We watched her walk back the long way. I wondered what the path through the woods was like—if it was anything at all like the one from my dreams— and if I'd ever feel brave enough to take it.

"Don't tell anyone about the doll," I told Anna the moment Vanessa was far enough away. "And definitely don't say we were in the woods."

It was a risk telling her that. She was really bad at keeping secrets, and even more so when she was told to keep them. But hopefully she understood how important this was.

"If you do, they'll take the doll away, and we'll never see Vanessa again."

"I don't want to go back there," Anna said. She took my hand and squeezed it tight, then started walking toward the house. "It was scary."

"Scary? You didn't want to leave."

She just shrugged and let go of my hand, skipping toward the house. Mom had just stepped out the front door, sun tea in her hands.

Sometimes my little sister could be so strange.

I stood there for a moment, watching the two of them talk. I felt a little silly, because I was jealous of Anna for getting a present from Vanessa. She was supposed to be *my* friend. But I knew the gift was, in a way, actually for me. This way I'd have the room to myself again, and my sister would be out of my hair. It was pretty genius. I was starting to realize that I had just gotten swept up in my grandmother's stories; there wasn't anything in the woods, there was no Beryl—if there had been, Vanessa surely would have mentioned her. It was all make-believe. It was all just a story my grandmother had made up and started to believe herself.

"Dinner's almost ready!" my mom called. My stomach rumbled; even though I'd had a few cookies, I was starving.

Then a breeze blew across my back, carrying the

sound of crackling leaves and snapped branches and the scent of old dirt.

That, and another sound. The sound of a woman hissing my name.

I didn't look back. I jogged all the way to the front door.

Even if it was just my imagination, I felt a lot safer inside.

18

"How was your friend's house?" Mom asked at dinner.

I looked at Anna, fully expecting her to talk about the dolls and how creepy it was.

But instead she said, "It was fun. Vanessa was really nice. Her aunt even made us cookies."

Mom tried to look disapproving, but she couldn't help but smile.

"Cookies before dinner?" she said. "That will ruin your appetite."

Anna answered by taking a big bite of lasagna

and making loud happy noises as she chewed. I rolled my eyes.

"What about you, Josie? Will you be hanging out with Vanessa more? She seemed very sweet. Maybe you could invite her over to dinner sometime."

I knew I should have felt happy that Mom was offering, but I didn't. I glanced at Grandma Jeannie, who was eating her food silently.

"Yeah," I said. "I thought maybe she could come over this weekend."

If she came over for a slumber party, there was a better chance we could just hide up in my room until Grandma went to sleep.

"That could be fun," Mom said.

"How about you?" I asked. "Any luck on your job hunt?"

Mom smiled again, but this time I could tell she was forcing it.

"Not yet," she said. "But that's okay. It's been good to catch up with your grandma."

"Beryl LeFarge is watching," Grandma said.

She had raised a forkful of lasagna to her lips but didn't bite it. Her hand shook. The food fell onto the plate.

"Nobody's watching us," Mom assured her. "It's just us here."

But Grandma wasn't having it. "*Beryl* is watching," she insisted. "She's angry. She's hungry. She'll attack soon."

Mom looked at me, and then at Anna, whose eyes were wide with fear. For some reason, I thought of the doll tucked safely in Anna's backpack.

"Mom—" my mom began.

Grandma stood up quickly, knocking over her chair and her glass, spilling sun tea all over the table.

"I have to protect you. I have to—"

Mom was there in a second. She put her hands on Grandma's shoulders.

"Come on, Mom. Let's get you to bed."

"Can't sleep. Beryl comes in the night. I hear her knocking against the windows. She's after the girls. She's mad I'm protecting them. She'll attack soon."

Mom led Grandma away, and Grandma muttered about Beryl the entire time. It was only when they had both left the room that I realized my own hands were shaking.

"Anna," I whispered.

But Anna didn't stick around—she jumped up from the table, grabbed her bookbag, and ran upstairs to her bedroom. I thought I heard her crying.

I sat there for a while. My hunger was gone and my hands wouldn't stop shaking. I couldn't stop looking out the window, at the coming sunset. *Beryl comes in the night.*

It was all just a story Grandma made up.

It was all just made up.

So why couldn't I stop staring out the window, for fear that someone was staring back?

Why, when I finally left the table and brought my plate into the kitchen, did I worry that tonight was the night I'd discover just how terrible this Beryl LeFarge really was?

Worse—why did I worry that, despite her assurance otherwise, Vanessa was somehow involved?

But that was ridiculous. Vanessa was my friend. She gave the doll to Anna to make her feel better. Vanessa was on our side.

Right?

19

I knew I was dreaming.

I knew it, but it didn't make me wake up. And the moment I realized that, I realized what sort of dream this was going to be.

I was in the woods. Running.

And I knew Beryl was running behind me. I could hear her footsteps in the trees. I could feel her rancid breath on my neck. I didn't look behind me—I knew if I did, I would trip and fall, and then she would have me.

Branches scratched my face and legs and hands as I ran. Some felt like they were covered in thorns, they hurt so bad.

I didn't focus on them.

I focused on running faster. *Faster.* My heart beating as fast as my footsteps, my throat as hot as Beryl's breath on the back of my neck.

She's catching up.

She's catching up.

"*Josieeeeeeeee.*"

Then the woods thinned out. The path led straight to where I knew it would: Vanessa's house.

I ran past the broken mannequins and doll-covered birdbaths. Up the front steps.

But no doll opened the door. Instead, the door was slightly ajar. I ran inside and slammed it shut behind me. My heart hammered so loud I could barely hear the beast behind me. Then the creature thundered up the porch and slammed into the door. Everything shook. A picture fell to the floor with a crash.

I pressed myself to the door to keep it from opening but it crashed again. Every hit made the house shake and my teeth chatter. I closed my eyes as tears fell and I wished the monster would stop.

Slam!

"Go away," I whispered.

Slam!

"Go away."

Slam!

"Go away!"

Then the crashing stopped.

I gasped at the sudden silence. It had worked—I was safe.

Then I opened my eyes. Truly saw where I was.

Dolls everywhere. Dolls facing the walls.

The smell of cookies burning.

As one, every doll along the hallway slowly turned its head to stare at me.

Except they weren't staring. Their eyes were crossed out with paint.

Their mouths were open.

They screamed—

20

I woke up covered in sweat. When I looked at my legs they were covered in scratches.

I blinked.

The scratches went away.

I reached down and rubbed my hands over my unscratched legs. My heart was pounding like I really *had* run through the woods. I tried to calm my nerves. I hadn't actually been scratched. It was like Anna thinking she was awake when she was really dreaming: I must have still been partly asleep when I thought I'd woken up. I put my hand to my rapidly beating heart. Was I going crazy?

Then my alarm buzzed loudly beside me. I turned it off and flopped back on my bed.

My empty bed.

I couldn't tell what I was feeling: relief that Anna had gone a whole night without coming into my room, or fear. Had she had a similar nightmare? Was she safe?

Beryl comes in the night, Grandma had said. *She'll attack soon.*

And I hadn't been around to protect Anna.

I pushed myself out of bed and ran to her door.

"Anna?" I asked. I knocked. She didn't answer.

She wasn't in her room.

I ran inside and looked around, tossed back her covers to make sure. But she wasn't sleeping.

No. No no no no. She can't have been taken!

"Anna?" I called, louder this time. My voice shook with panic.

Mom came in the door and looked in, sleepy and confused.

"Josie, what's wrong?"

"Anna! She's missing."

"She's downstairs having breakfast," Mom said. "Are you feeling okay?"

I was panting. When I looked in the mirror, I saw that my face was flushed and my hair was wild.

"I . . ."

But I didn't have anything to say. How could I explain that I was worried that Anna had been taken by a creature from Grandma's stories? We looked at each other for a long time. Once, Mom and I had talked about everything. Now I had more secrets than I could count. It felt like—even though we were only standing a few feet apart—we were living in completely different cities.

"Sorry," I muttered. "Bad dreams."

Mom stepped in and knelt in front of me. She put the back of her hand on my cheek and then my forehead.

"Are you sure you're feeling okay, honey?" she asked. "You haven't been acting like yourself since we moved here."

My fear over Anna being gone suddenly snapped to anger.

"That's because I didn't want to move here!" I reminded her. "I hate it."

Mom's eyes tightened.

"I'm sorry, Josie. I know this is hard on you, but it was the only choice."

"No. We could have gotten a smaller place in the city. You could have gotten another job. We didn't *have* to leave Chicago. You wanted to go. But you didn't ask us. You never ask us anything!"

"Josie, that's not fair."

Not fair?

Not fair was worrying about getting eaten by a monster or losing my sister when, a week ago, the only things I worried about were ignoring creepy people on my walk home or missing the bus. Now I was having nightmares about monsters and my grandma was going crazy and maybe I was, too, and everything was terrible. She had no idea what wasn't fair.

The worst part was that I couldn't tell her about any of it. Just like I couldn't tell Vanessa without risking scaring her off. And I couldn't tell any friends back home because there was no way they'd understand.

I wouldn't understand, if I wasn't the one living it.

It wasn't until Mom wiped a tear from my cheek that I realized I was crying from frustration.

"I know this is hard—" she began again, but I cut her off.

"No. You don't." Then I stormed out of the room and downstairs.

I didn't stop until I was out on the back porch, where Grandma Jeannie was standing again by the railing, a mug of tea forgotten in her hands.

"Beryl is hungry," she said as a way of greeting.

"I'm sick of hearing about Beryl!" I yelled. I slammed my hands on the railing.

Grandma Jeannie looked at me for a long time. She didn't speak. So I filled the silence.

"It's all made up, Grandma. Mom said your brain is playing tricks on you and it's not real. Beryl isn't real."

Grandma continued to look at me.

"Beryl *is* real," she said, her voice terrifyingly calm. "And you will know soon enough. She's taken another child."

21

Vanessa was waiting for me at school. Well, waiting for us.

Anna and I hopped out of the car and waved good-bye to Mom—it had been an awkward, quiet car ride after my outburst earlier. Vanessa was at our side before Mom had even pulled out of the driveway.

"How's it going?" Vanessa asked.

Maybe it was my imagination, but she seemed a little down. I wondered if she was sad that we'd left so quickly yesterday. Or maybe it was just the weather—the sky had grown overcast during the short drive to school, and the wind that blew was cold and hinted at secrets.

"Okay," I lied.

"Josie got in a fight with Mom this morning," Anna said. I glared at her.

"It wasn't because you visited, was it?" Vanessa asked.

I shook my head.

"It's because she doesn't want to live here anymore," Anna replied.

"*Anna.*"

But Vanessa just smiled sadly.

"I understand. I fought with my aunt a lot when I moved here. It takes a while to get used to, especially when you're from a city." She looked from me to Anna. "How did you sleep?"

"Great!" Anna replied. "I didn't have nightmares at all."

I didn't want to admit my own nightmares. Or that I was angry at Anna for sleeping well when this was the third night I hadn't slept.

Thankfully, I didn't have to say anything—the

first bell rang and kids started crowding into the school.

"How are *you* doing?" I asked Vanessa as we filed in.

She shrugged.

"My aunt wasn't in a good mood last night," she said.

"Because of us?"

"No," she replied. But it came a second too late. I knew she was lying. "She was sad she didn't get to meet you, though."

"Well, my mom said you should come over to our place sometime. Maybe this weekend?"

Vanessa smiled, but it seemed a little sad.

"That's really sweet of you. I'd love to." It didn't sound like she meant it.

I tried to tell myself that having her over would be okay, but all I could think of was Grandma Jeannie's stories and rules. If only I could take Vanessa back to my real home in Chicago. Back with my friends and my favorite places, where I could escape whenever my family got too strange.

Now it felt like there was nowhere to run.

"What's wrong?" Vanessa asked.

"I just . . . I miss home."

"Me too," Vanessa replied sadly. She patted my shoulder consolingly.

For some reason, she sounded sadder than I've ever felt in my whole life.

22

I knew something was wrong after lunch.

I was in class and the teacher took attendance. I wasn't paying attention, but I started to when he repeated the name a few times and another student called out, "She's not here!"

"Did she tell anyone she wasn't going to be in today?" the teacher asked.

"No," the original speaker said. I think her name was Cindy. "But she didn't show up to social studies this morning either. Maybe she's sick."

That wasn't what was strange, though—people were sick all the time. The teacher made a quick call to the office and then continued class. It wasn't until the principal walked in, about halfway through class, that we learned something was really wrong.

"Students," the principal said. "I'd like to ask you a few questions."

Everyone went quiet immediately. Even the rowdy kids paid attention—Principal Overton was known for harsh punishment.

"Has anyone seen Karen Little today?" she asked.

No one raised their hand.

"Are you sure?"

Again, no one answered.

"Because I have just gotten off the phone with her parents. They say she left for school this morning."

The silence grew heavier with every word as we realized what she was saying.

"She was last seen walking into the woods," Principal Overton said. "If any of you can think of anything, please come to me directly. Hopefully this will all be taken care of soon."

I was shocked when she left.

Did they think Karen Little had been taken? Or that she was skipping school? I didn't know her at all, but from the few classes we'd had together, she didn't seem like the rebel type. She always sat in the front and answered questions. What surprised me was how the principal was handling this. Why weren't the cops involved? Why had she asked the class as a whole? If this had been in Chicago, we'd all have been questioned individually. I couldn't tell if this was a big deal or if this was just another occurrence.

I remembered Grandma Jeannie's final words: *She's taken another child.*

I tried to convince myself this was ridiculous. Karen was just skipping school and hadn't told anyone. The fact that she was last seen going into the woods . . . most of this town was covered by the woods. I'd seen dozens of kids cut through there for shortcuts or to hang out. It wasn't strange.

But it did make chills rush across my skin.

No. I wasn't going to let my grandma affect me at school, too. This was the only place her ramblings and rules didn't apply. I wouldn't let myself believe her wild tales.

Still, I couldn't focus the rest of the day. And when we were finally let out, there were cop cars outside the school. Well, two cop cars. For a town this small, that felt like a lot.

The cops were questioning a few kids and some parents as well.

"I guess that means she didn't show up," Vanessa said.

I jumped. I hadn't heard her come up to me.

"I guess," I said. "Did you know her?"

Vanessa shrugged and watched the cop cars.

"Not really. We had a few classes together."

"The principal said she was last seen in the woods."

"That's because the woods are everywhere." She gestured to the school grounds, which were ringed by the forest. Then she looked at me with a little grin. "Don't tell me you think that the monster got her."

I shook my head. "Don't be silly. I don't believe in that."

"Right." I could tell she was giving me a hard time. Thankfully, she changed the subject. "Do you still want me to come over this weekend?"

"Yeah. It'll be fun. But I'll warn you—we still

don't have any internet. So we just have board games and stuff like that."

"That's okay. We'll get to know each other better."

Anna came up behind us and gave me a hug. Then she hugged Vanessa.

"Vanessa said she'll come over this weekend," I said.

"Yay!" Anna said. Then she paused. "But aren't you worried she'll get bored?"

"I'm sure we'll find something to do," Vanessa said. "If nothing else, we can always tell ghost stories." She winked.

23

Karen Little never showed up. Either at school or at home.

Rumors began circulating. Even though I didn't have any real friends beyond Vanessa, I still heard the talk in the hallways: Some kids thought she'd run away. Others thought she'd been abducted. I tried to ignore those. I didn't want to think about something so terrible happening. Not in a town like this.

About the only good thing was that Anna had stopped having nightmares.

Although she needed to stop playing tricks on me.

I swore I heard her come into my room at night and giggle. When I turned on the lights, though, she had already run out and pretended to be asleep. I confronted her about it a few times, but she was as good a liar as she was bad at keeping secrets: She flat-out refused to admit that she'd come into my room at all. She even went so far as to start crying when I refused to believe her. And then she played a very mean trick.

I woke up to my alarm like usual.

From bad dreams. As usual.

I didn't open my eyes when I reached to turn the alarm off. My hand smacked into something small and hard.

I blinked open my eyes and nearly screamed.

It was the doll Vanessa had given Anna.

It sat there on my bedside table, right next to my alarm. Its face was pointed directly at me. For some reason, that creepy smile made my skin crawl.

I couldn't remember its smile being that wide before.

I shook my head and knocked the doll on its face.

Anna was playing tricks, probably for attention.

Which just meant I needed to ignore her. And I needed to stop letting my imagination get away from me. Otherwise, soon, I'd be just as bad as Grandma Jeannie.

That was the other thing—Grandma Jeannie had gotten worse. Much worse. Now that Karen Little had been reported missing, Grandma doubled down on her strange rules and muttering. It made Mom upset, but no matter what she tried, she couldn't get Grandma to calm down. Grandma Jeannie came into our rooms to make sure our windows were closed. She watched us from the back porch whenever Anna and I went outside. She checked our closets. She never told us what she was looking for, but I knew: She was making sure we weren't hiding a doll anywhere.

Which just made me angrier that Anna would risk getting us both in a lot of trouble—and potentially getting me banned from ever seeing my new best friend again—by leaving the doll on my nightstand.

When I got up, I grabbed the doll and stuffed it inside a pillowcase, then stormed into Anna's room. She was still in bed.

"Why would you do this?" I asked. I tried to keep my voice down, but it was impossible to keep the anger from my words.

"What?" she asked innocently, looking at the pillowcase with confusion.

I tossed it on her bed. She reached out for it.

"This. Why would you put this in my room?" I lowered my voice even more. "You know how much trouble we'd be in if Grandma saw it! Vanessa is coming over tomorrow night—do you want to get us all in trouble?"

Rather than throwing a fit like she usually did when she got caught, tears welled up in Anna's eyes. She looked from the doll in her trembling hand to me.

"I didn't do it," she whimpered. "I just woke up!"

"Don't lie to me," I said. "I know you did it. How else did it get in my room? You've been coming in every night to try to scare me. Now I've had it. If you do it again, I'm telling Mom. And then you'll be grounded for sure."

Tears rolled down her face. It took a lot of control not to give in and go over to wipe them away—mad as I was, I hated seeing her cry. Then again, she probably knew that. She was probably trying to use that against me. Just the thought of it made me angrier.

"Stay out of my room, Anna," I said firmly.

"I haven't been in your room," she whispered, but I was already out the door.

I was mad—really mad—but it didn't stop her words from sinking in. I knew she was lying. She had to be.

There was no other way the doll could have gotten into my room.

24

Vanessa was in an unusually cheerful mood at school. Even though everyone else seemed on edge or upset, she was smiling when I sat down next to her at lunch.

"Aunt Tilda made us more cookies!" she said, opening her lunch bag and pulling out at least a dozen chocolate chip treats.

I was still upset over the morning, also because Mom gave Anna and me a speech on the way to school along the lines of "be on your best behavior tonight." I knew what she meant—don't do anything that would upset Grandma. The trouble was, I didn't know what would or wouldn't upset Grandma anymore—except any mention of Karen Little. Besides, if anyone needed that talk, it was Anna. She was the one risking everything by leaving her stupid doll out.

The sight of the cookies made my anger fade just a little bit.

"What's wrong?" Vanessa asked. Even though we'd only known each other a short time, she was already really good at telling my mood. Or maybe I was just really bad at hiding things.

I almost told her about my mom and about Anna, but I didn't want to say anything that might make her not want to come over.

"Nothing," I said. "I didn't sleep much."

She looked at me for a while, then passed me the cookies.

"Well, I don't think we'll be sleeping much tomorrow either, so you better eat a lot of sugar now."

I tried to smile and took a cookie.

"Why? What did you want to do?"

"We're going to tell ghost stories," she said. "I have a lot of good ones."

I rolled my eyes. "Ghost stories are for little kids."

"They are not!" she said with an exaggerated pout. "You're just saying that because you know you'll be scared."

They couldn't be any scarier than what Grandma Jeannie had been telling us lately.

"Why are you in such a good mood?" I asked. And then, because that sounded rude, I added, "Or is it just the cookies?"

She laughed and bit down on another cookie—I wondered if she'd packed anything else for lunch.

"I'm just excited to have a sleepover," she said. "I haven't had a friend like you since I moved here."

What I saw in that flicker of her eyes wasn't excitement. It was sadness. And fear.

That's when I wondered . . . was Vanessa lying to me, too, like Anna was? And if so, what was she keeping secret?

25

Grandma Jeannie didn't join us at dinner when Vanessa came over Saturday night.

I felt bad she wasn't doing well, but I was also sort of relieved, which made me feel even worse. It meant I didn't have to worry about her saying anything strange to Vanessa, or demanding to search her bag for a doll before she came into the house.

Mom made homemade pizzas—she made the dough from scratch and everything—and let us put whatever toppings we wanted on our halves. I just put extra cheese on mine. Vanessa loaded hers with veggies. And Anna made a big smiley face out of pepperoni on hers. We listened to music in the kitchen while the pizzas cooked, and Mom asked Vanessa about her experiences living here.

Vanessa answered everything smoothly, like she was talking to a friend and not an adult. She even shared things that I hadn't gotten to ask her yet, like what her parents did (lawyers) and why she was allowed to take care of her aunt all by herself (her parents were too busy). Eventually, though, Vanessa turned the conversation around like she always did, and started asking Mom her own questions.

"What was it like when you lived here?" Vanessa asked.

Mom laughed and ate a piece of raw green pepper—even though I loved vegetables, I thought it was a little gross.

"Almost the same as it is now," she replied. "I think Hank at the general store hasn't aged a day."

"I think that's because he's always been older than dirt," Vanessa replied.

I raised an eyebrow. I thought that was a phrase only adults said.

Mom just laughed again. It was cut short when Anna asked a very strange question.

"Were any kids taken when you were a little girl, Momma?"

We all went silent. The only sound in the kitchen was the radio, and even that seemed quiet.

"Why would you ask that, honey?" Mom said. I couldn't tell if she was shocked or angry about Anna's question. She didn't seem to want to answer either way.

"My friend Clara mentioned it at school today. *She* says she heard that there were a lot of disappearances here, a long time ago."

I watched Mom intently. She bit her lip, then quickly turned to check the pizza.

She didn't answer.

"Mom?" Anna asked.

"Yes, honey?" Mom sounded exasperated.

Anna repeated her question.

Mom paused. Then, finally, she admitted the truth.

"Yes," she said. My stomach turned to ice.

"How many?"

I wanted to push her for asking these questions with Vanessa in the room—this was the sort of thing to talk about in private. Thankfully, Mom felt the same way. She looked at Vanessa with concern. She probably didn't want Vanessa telling her aunt that we were discussing missing kids at dinner. That wasn't the sort of thing people talked about around guests.

"A few," Mom replied.

"Is that why Grandma sent you to a private school?" Anna asked. "She didn't want you to get taken?"

"Anna!" I blurted out. Even though I wanted to find out the answer, I didn't want to have this conversation in front of Vanessa. She must really think my family was crazy. Just wait until she met Grandma Jeannie.

"What?" Anna asked innocently. "I want to know."

"It's okay," Mom said. She sighed and looked at Vanessa. "But I think this is something we should talk about later."

Finally, someone was seeing sense.

"Don't mind me," Vanessa said. "I'm curious, too."

Despite her casual tone, something in her expression made me think she actually was bothered by what we were talking about. I couldn't blame her. To know that Karen wasn't the first kid to go missing was one thing. To learn there had been others—maybe many others—was much scarier, even if it was years ago.

"No," I said, "let's talk about something else. We'll leave the ghost stories for later."

"Ghost stories? You mean the kids *died*?" Anna asked.

"Anna!" I yelled again. "Cut it out."

Anna pouted. Sometimes she asked way too many questions. It didn't help that I wanted to know the answers. I knew, though, that Mom would never tell us that. She would think we were too young to deal with something horrible like that.

Mom tried to keep the conversation light, but Anna kept finding ways to ask about missing children. Finally, Mom got flustered and asked why Anna wanted to know so badly.

Anna said it was because of her new friend, Clara.

Mom said maybe Clara wasn't as good a friend as Anna thought, and she wanted to have a talk with Clara's parents.

Anna said Clara didn't have parents.

I wondered aloud if Anna was just making Clara up, since I still hadn't met her.

That just made Anna leave the table angrily.

Mom told me I had been rude, but I could also tell she was relieved that Anna had stopped asking questions. Vanessa tried to steer the conversation toward some of the locals again, but I stopped listening. All I could hear was Anna stomping around in her room above us.

The good part of this was that when dinner was over, Vanessa and I could go back to my room without me having to figure out how to get rid of Anna. When Mom asked what we were going to do, I said we'd be playing board games. We even took out an old game of Chutes and Ladders that Grandma had around. In truth, though, we were mostly just pushing the pieces around and talking. It was hard for me to concentrate on anything after that dinner.

"So the doll worked?" Vanessa asked me out of the blue.

"What do you mean?"

"I mean," Vanessa said, "your sister hasn't come in here since then, right?"

"Nope," I said. "She hasn't had nightmares again."

"Have you?"

I'd hoped she wasn't going to ask. I was so bad at lying.

"Yes," I admitted.

"Really? What about?"

She crossed her legs and looked at me intently. I almost expected her to pull out a notebook so she could write it all down, like she was my counselor. I hadn't seen a counselor since the weeks following Mom and Dad's divorce two years ago.

I looked at the game board and considered not answering. But Vanessa was the only girl here who talked to me. I couldn't cut her out like that.

"The woods," I muttered. I moved my game piece.

I almost expected Vanessa to laugh. Instead, she made a "hmm" noise under her breath. Maybe she was just thinking about her next move. But when I looked up, she was still staring at me like she was trying to figure me out.

"I guess that makes sense," she said. "The woods are a scary place. Especially if your grandma is telling you ghost stories about them."

I shrugged. I wanted her to move so we could talk about something else. What else was there to talk about, though? It wasn't like either of us had any gossip.

Suddenly, my big empty room seemed even bigger and emptier than before.

"So what happens in your bad dreams?" Vanessa asked.

I kept expecting her to make fun of me, even though she had never, ever done so. Even my best friends in Chicago would have joked about me having nightmares, and how that was for little kids. I was old enough not to be afraid of the dark or believe the boogieman was real.

But Vanessa was still looking at me seriously, as though nothing I could say would surprise her or make her laugh. It was weird.

It reminded me of how my counselor had looked at me, and all the other adults when they would ask if I was okay in the wake of the divorce.

"Well," I said. She still hadn't moved her game piece, so I had no choice but to talk and wait. "I'm always running from something. A monster. And then . . ."

"Yeah?"

"It's stupid."

"I'm sure it's not."

"I find your house."

"Really?" She leaned back and bit her lip like she was thinking. "That's kind of creepy."

"Yeah." I looked away. There's no way I'd tell her what happened when I got to her dream house—she didn't need to know about the doll that looked like her. And she definitely didn't need to know that I'd seen her house in my dream before I'd ever visited.

She laughed. Not like she was making fun of me, but like she was trying to make the situation less scary.

"Well, I can understand why you wouldn't want to come over to my house again. But," she said, moving her game piece closer to the finish line, "you have to admit my aunt bakes some pretty good cookies."

"Maybe someday I'll get to meet her."

I rolled the dice and moved forward, but not very far.

Then she rolled the dice and got to the finish line.

"Maybe," she said. She looked at me, then back to the game she'd just easily won. "I'm really glad I met you, Josie."

"Me too," I replied. "School would be horrible without you."

She smiled sadly. "It's more than that. It's been really lonely here. I'm glad I finally made a friend."

It wasn't the first time she'd said that, but it still made me feel good inside. Clearly, I hadn't scared her off with my strange family.

"It's sad, though," she said, almost to herself.

"What is?" I asked.

"I want you to stay here so we can keep being friends. But I know you don't want to be in this town. I guess I can't blame you."

"Maybe one day we can run away together," I

said. I was joking. When she looked at me, though, she was serious.

"I can't get out of here," she said. Her words were choked. She shook her head and looked back to the game, even though it was over. "I just mean . . . until my aunt is better, I can't leave her side."

"I still think it stinks that your parents aren't taking care of her."

She nodded to herself.

"It does. Sometimes I feel really alone."

She sounded like she was on the verge of crying. I reached out and put my hand on her arm. Her skin was always so cold.

"Me too. But maybe now we don't have to feel that way. You've got a friend now." I tried to laugh. "Besides, it sounds like I'll be here for a while."

"Yeah," she said, her voice still sad. "I think you will be, too."

26

"You're going to love it here," Vanessa said.

Her voice sounded different. Like she was talking to me from the bottom of a well. Even though she was standing right next to me in the hallway, she sounded so very far away.

The hallway.

The hallway in Beryl's house.

My skin went cold. Wait, how could I be cold in the dream? I looked behind me, hoping to find the door, but the hallway stretched out forever into darkness.

That's when I realized there weren't any dolls in the hall. And Vanessa wasn't doll-like.

My panic started to ease up. Maybe this wasn't a nightmare after all. Maybe it was just a normal dream. But if it was a normal dream, why was I realizing it was a dream at all?

"Come on," Vanessa said. She took my hand. Her fingers were terribly cold on my skin. And firm. She started walking down the hall, and I had no choice but to follow.

We seemed to walk forever, but the hall didn't change and the doors we passed remained closed.

"Where are we going?" I asked. My voice shook. Even if this wasn't scary, it was hard to believe it wasn't a nightmare. Her voice was so distant, and as cold as her fingers.

"To your room," she said.

"I have a room," I said, my words faltering.

"Your new room, in your new home." She looked over and smiled at me. Her eyes were glassy as a doll's. "Your new friends are waiting."

My feet stumbled. I didn't like the way she said it.

Despite my hesitation, we kept walking. I couldn't stop if I wanted to.

We passed by a door that wasn't fully closed. The door was covered in locks. Inside was a glass case, but I didn't get the chance to see what was inside it before being dragged away.

"What's in there?" I asked.

"Nothing," Vanessa replied. She gripped my hand tighter and pulled faster.

Soon we were running, and the hall kept stretching on and on, and my skin was coated with sweat, not just because I was out of shape, but because there was something running up behind us. Something growling.

Something chasing us.

I knew then exactly what it was.

Beryl had gotten inside!

I ran faster.

We had to hide.

We had to find safety.

But the hallways stretched on and on and all the doors were locked and I could feel Beryl now in the hallway with us. So close. So close. I knew that if I looked behind us, whatever I saw would be so terrifying I would freeze up. I could feel it in my bones.

A door at the end of the hall opened.

We rushed in. My heart wanted to pound out of my chest.

It wasn't until the door slammed shut behind us that I realized we weren't any safer in here.

There was a reason there were no dolls in the hallway. They were all in the room.

Locked in. With us.

The beast chasing us thudded into the door with a crash.

SLAM!

SLAM!

SLAM!

Vanessa leaned against it. She was panting.

"Don't worry," she said, her voice somehow calm despite her ragged breath. "You're safe in here. This is your room. You'll always be safe from her in your room."

And it *was* my room. It had the same high ceilings. The same bare walls. The same big bed. Except in here, the floor was carpeted with dolls. All of them lying broken and mismatched like there had been a terrible accident.

They weren't what made me forget about the monster outside.

On my bed was a life-size doll.

Blonde hair in ringlets. Brown eyes.

She looked exactly like Karen Little.

"Let's be friends. Forever," the doll said. She smiled, and her face cracked.

Vanessa's hand clamped over my mouth. Before I could scream, the room went dark.

27

Vanessa slept like a rock.

I woke up before her to the smell of Mom brewing coffee in the kitchen, which always woke me up. I had slept so well. Which was strange, because I usually couldn't sleep at all during sleepovers. But if I slept well, Vanessa must have slept even better.

She lay there, still as a statue, on her back, and for a moment I wondered if she was even breathing. Then I saw her chest move, and that made me look at the locket she always wore. I found it strange that she even wore it to bed. It was simple tarnished gold. Nothing really cool, and it always seemed to clash with what she was wearing at school, but maybe that was why she wore it. To make her stand out because she didn't match.

Something about it seemed off, though.

And something about *that* made me want to reach out and touch it. Which was weird, because I was there staring at my new friend while she was asleep. What if she woke up and saw me watching?

I turned over and looked at the nightstand. I was relieved to find that there wasn't any doll sitting beside my alarm clock. I guessed that Anna hadn't been brave enough to try sneaking in while Vanessa was staying over. Either that, or she was so upset she'd quit trying. I hoped it was the latter; I didn't want to have to keep fighting her about it.

I sat up. Vanessa didn't move.

I stretched. Still no movement.

For a moment I considered just trying to fall back asleep, but I could hear Mom clattering around in the kitchen now, and if today was anything like the days back in Chicago when I had friends over, that meant she was going to be making chocolate chip pancakes for breakfast. And I couldn't miss that.

I gave Vanessa a little shake.

She didn't move.

I tried again, this time saying her name.

Again, no movement. Her skin was cold, and even though I knew she was breathing, it still creeped me out.

Finally, I gave her a big shake and called her name even louder. I expected her to wake up with a screech—that's what I would have done. But she just blinked open her eyes like she was being gently woken from a nap.

So weird.

"Good morning," she said. And just like that she sat up and was wide awake. *So* weird.

We went and brushed our teeth, and then went down for breakfast. I was right—Mom had made chocolate chip pancakes. Anna was already sitting at the table, playing with her teddy bear. Grandma Jeannie wasn't there, and she wasn't on the back patio either. Maybe she was still in bed.

Suddenly, I felt guilty that I'd been happy she was away last night. What if she was getting really sick?

Then Mom served up the pancakes, and my guilt vanished.

Once more, Vanessa asked all the questions. Mom seemed more than happy to talk about things, so we spent the morning telling Vanessa about Chicago and some of the shows we'd seen, and the type of job Mom was looking for, and how long Mom thought we would stay here.

That made me pause and listen carefully.

How long *was* Mom thinking of keeping us here? She'd never admitted anything before.

"I don't know," Mom eventually said.

"What do you mean?" Vanessa asked casually.

"Well, it depends on how my mom is doing. And if I can get a job back in Chicago." She paused. "Or here."

My mouth fell open. The way she said it made it sound like she was actually planning on staying here not just for the rest of the school year, but forever.

I couldn't imagine Mom ever finding a job in a town this small that would make her happy—she used to work with a big investment firm in Chicago, and she said she loved it. I couldn't imagine this place offering anything like that. And yet, I also had no doubt that she would stay here for Grandma.

I looked at Vanessa. She looked at me. I could tell we were having the same thought.

On the one hand, we were happy that we got to be friends for a while.

On the other, it felt like both of us were trapped.

28

It was after breakfast when Grandma Jeannie came down.

Vanessa and I were in the backyard, playing on the swing set while Mom and Anna cleaned up. (Anna definitely didn't want to help, but Mom made her.) I knew before the porch door even opened that it was Grandma Jeannie. I knew, because Vanessa immediately stopped swinging. She went as stiff as when she had been sleeping.

When I turned and looked at Grandma, she was just as still as Vanessa. She had her cane in one hand and a sun tea in the other.

"How . . . how . . ." Grandma stuttered. "You shouldn't be here. She shouldn't . . ."

Vanessa clicked into action then. She looked from Grandma Jeannie to me.

"I should go," she said. She hopped off the swing.

"No, wait," I said. "It's okay."

"I . . ."

But Vanessa didn't complete her sentence. At that moment, Grandma Jeannie dropped her glass. It shattered to the porch, making me jump.

"How are you . . ." Grandma kept repeating. I couldn't focus on her, though. Vanessa was already running, but not toward the patio or the house. She was running straight into the woods.

"Vanessa!" I called.

She didn't stop or look back. I watched her go. I knew she was going home, but it almost looked like she was some wild creature, running into the forest for safety from a predator.

I turned back to Grandma. I didn't know if I wanted to yell at her for scaring off my friend or ask her what was wrong.

I didn't get the chance.

"It's happening again," she said, just loud enough for me to hear.

Then she fell to the ground.

29

We were up in Grandma Jeannie's room. The doctor was there at her bedside, talking to Mom. Anna was at the foot of the bed, holding her teddy bear tight to her chest.

I watched Grandma nervously. The doctor said she would be okay, that she'd just fainted from shock and hadn't broken anything. At worst, she'd have a few bruises.

"She needs a lot of rest and fluids," the doctor said. "If you need anything else, I'm just down the road."

Then she grabbed her bag of medical supplies and left.

I'd never seen a doctor come to someone's house before. I guess it was a little comforting that they did that. Though it was also a little worrying that they didn't seem to have a big hospital. Which just made me wonder . . . where had Vanessa's aunt gotten knee surgery?

That made me think of Vanessa running away. I wished I had a way to call her and ask her what was up. Her running like that made me angry, but also kind of sad. I didn't know who I was angriest with: Grandma for freaking out, or Vanessa for running off. Maybe I was maddest at myself for letting any of this happen in the first place.

I *knew* having a friend over would be a bad idea. I knew everything in this town was a bad idea.

It was only when Mom put her hand on my shoulder and led me out of the bedroom into my own that I realized I was crying.

"Honey, what's wrong?" she asked.

I opened my mouth, but how could I tell her the

truth? That I felt responsible for Grandma fainting? That I was so angry about living here I wanted to run away? That Vanessa was the only friend I had, and she would probably never talk to me again?

Everything felt like my fault. And *nothing* felt like my fault.

All I could do was cry harder.

Mom held me close and ran her fingers through my hair.

"I'm so sorry you had to go through all this, honey. But Grandma will be okay. I promise you, everything will be okay."

Even then, I knew it was a lie.

30

I couldn't focus the rest of the day.

Anna spent the morning playing in the backyard, and I spent the time cleaning up my bedroom. It didn't need it, but there was nothing else to do besides homework, and I really didn't want to do *that*. The problem was, cleaning my room just made me think of Vanessa staying the night. I wished I had other friends. I wished there was a way to talk to my friends back home. I could invite them out here, but I knew they'd never come—not when they would be too busy doing fun things. Who could blame them? I wouldn't come out here if I didn't have to.

By the time I was done cleaning, I felt so sorry for myself I nearly just wandered into the woods to find Vanessa or get lost.

I knew that would be a bad move, and I was also still a little upset that Vanessa had run off on me. She'd even left her overnight bag here. I'd have to bring it with me to school tomorrow.

Hopefully that meant she'd still talk to me.

I sat on my bed for a while and stared out the window. Anna was still playing out there, content with the world. I didn't know how she did it; she actually seemed kind of happy here. And I was miserable. I thought about reading but didn't have any books I could sink into. We still didn't have cable, and I had watched all the movies I'd brought with me a dozen times.

Ugh. If every weekend was like this, I was going to die of boredom.

After a while, I hopped off the bed and left my room. Mom was cleaning, and I figured it was almost lunchtime, so I would make myself a snack.

As I was passing Grandma's room, I heard her

cough. I paused. I wanted to ask her what had happened with Vanessa, and why she'd acted so strangely. I also didn't want to make her any worse. Then Grandma moaned a little, like she was hurt, and I jogged into her room.

Save for the time with the doctor that morning, I'd never spent much time in here. It was a simple room, with a few photos of our family—portraits of Mom and Anna and me, old photos of Grandma and Grandpa on their wedding day or on vacation. There were no other decorations, and it always made me a little sad. It was just so empty.

Grandma was curled up in bed. She looked tiny, the thin covers pulled around her and the ceiling fan spinning slowly. Often, her room smelled like flowers and perfume. Right now, it smelled stale, like old breath.

For some reason, it reminded me of the way Vanessa's house smelled in my nightmares.

"Grandma?" I asked.

She rolled her head to look at me, blinking with tired eyes.

"Josie?" she asked.

Her voice was barely more than a whisper. All she'd done was fall, yet she looked so incredibly sick. I felt even worse now for ever being angry with her. She *was* sick. It was so easy to forget that when she looked or acted normal.

"Yes, Grandma," I said. "Are you okay?"

I stepped up to her bedside.

She didn't just look sick—she looked *ancient*. She'd always had a brightness in her eyes and smile, and now that brightness was dimmed.

"Who . . . who was that girl today?"

"Her name's Vanessa, Grandma. She's my friend." Then, despite myself, I thought, *Until you scared her off by yelling at her.*

Grandma shook her head.

"Can't be . . . can't be . . ." She moaned again and rolled over.

"Can't be what, Grandma?"

But she didn't answer. She just curled in on herself like she was scared.

"Grandma?" I asked. "Why did you—"

"Beryl is coming!" she shrieked, finding an energy I didn't know she still had. She turned over and grabbed my arm, looking me right in the eyes. "You've brought her in here. I can't protect you. Not anymore."

"Vanessa isn't Beryl," I said. I tried to wrench free from her grip, but her fingers were strong. "I don't know why you're so upset. She's my friend. She's just a girl."

"She's already gotten to you," Grandma said. She let go and sunk back into the pillows, looking even tinier and more tired than before. She started to cry. "Beryl will get you. I'm tired. So tired. I can't protect you any longer."

I didn't know why, but something in me snapped. Maybe it was because I *knew* that Grandma was sick, and that this was all in her head, and that it was causing *very real* problems outside of this bedroom.

"Beryl isn't real, Grandma!" I yelled. "Stop acting like there's a monster outside, when the only monster here is you!"

I turned and stormed out the door.

She called my name.

I didn't stop.

I kept walking down the hall.

That's when I realized she wasn't asking me to stop or to apologize.

"Stay out of the woods!" she was calling. "Beryl is coming for you!"

31

I didn't want to stay at home any longer.

Mom was in the kitchen doing dishes. She must not have heard me and Grandma, but she did notice how angry I was as I stormed past.

"Honey, what's wrong?" she asked.

I didn't answer.

There was so much anger inside of me that I knew if I stopped and talked, I would just start yelling things I would regret. I didn't know where I was going, only that I had to go *somewhere*.

I stormed out the front door and toward the road. Mom was behind me. She called out that I had to come back, but I wasn't listening. I wasn't going to listen to anyone, not any longer.

I knew I was going to get in trouble but I didn't care. What was the worst that could happen? They'd ground me? I already had enough weird rules to follow, and it's not like they could keep me from watching TV or going online when I couldn't do that anyway. My anger gave me a sort of clarity: I was already trapped. And that meant getting in trouble couldn't make anything any worse.

I was down the road when I realized where I was going. There weren't too many places nearby, so I guess it wasn't much of a surprise.

My feet were leading me straight toward Vanessa's.

I was going to go and apologize and tell her that we should really run away together. We could go to a big city where the stupid adults in our lives could never find us, and we would have fun and not be stuck out here in the woods.

I really thought that Mom would drive by and make me stop walking. Maybe she realized I needed to be out of the house. Maybe she realized there were too many rules. Or maybe she knew the truth, that I was going to go talk to Vanessa after she'd run off.

Or maybe she just knew that I was angry, and that she needed to let me blow off some steam.

It didn't matter. In no time at all, after not being passed by a single car, I was on the side path that led to Vanessa's house.

The woods were once again thick and quiet here, heavy. Like everything was waiting and watching me pass. The woods were eerie, but they were just woods.

There weren't any ghosts to come out and scare me in the light of day, no monsters waiting in the bushes. And every step was another reminder that I'd been lied to all this time, that we were all just playing along to keep Grandma from feeling bad.

I didn't want to play make-believe anymore. Not when it was ruining my life.

After what seemed like no time at all, I reached Vanessa's house.

It was definitely much cooler in the glade, and the air smelled heavy. No scents of baking today. No cookies or cinnamon.

The air smelled a lot like Grandma's bedroom.

Suddenly, I realized just how stupid I was for coming out here on my own. I stopped walking. The air was gravely silent. I could hear everything, though there wasn't anything to hear.

Until I *did* hear something, and it made my skin go cold.

Crying.

Vanessa.

I walked slowly to the front door, my feet crunching way too loudly on the dead leaves and sticks, trying to avoid stepping on the doll heads that had fallen on the path. Her crying got louder.

That's when I heard a voice.

Her voice.

I knew it from the way my blood ran cold.

Beryl.

"I grow hungry," Beryl rasped, her voice crawling down my spine on centipede feet. "You must bring me another."

"I can't," Vanessa said through her tears. "Please, just let me go."

"You can, and you will. Or else . . ."

Vanessa cried out again. I'd never heard someone sound so scared.

I didn't know what to do. Should I knock on the door? Should I run and get the police?

Before I could think, an angry growl sounded on the other side of the door.

"Perhaps you are lucky. I smell a child."

My body kicked into action.

I didn't think.

I ran.

In my rush, I tripped on a doll head and stumbled into one of the birdbaths, knocking more doll heads to the ground. They should have scattered every-where, but instead they stayed where they landed. And then, slowly, they turned . . . dead eyes zeroing in on me. I froze in terror.

"*Josieeee* . . ." Beryl hissed from somewhere that felt like it was inside my head.

My body kicked into action. I ran straight for the road, over the doll heads. I felt them smash under my feet. I felt them crying out.

Their cries didn't stop until I was safe on the road.

32

I ran all the way home, my blood pounding in my ears so hard that I couldn't think.

My brain was a mixed-up mess. Beryl was real. *Beryl was real.* I didn't know how I knew that the voice inside was Beryl's, but I did. It sounded like the creature that had been hissing outside my window, the voice that had chased me in my dreams.

Only now, in the daylight, I wasn't being chased.

I ran until I reached my front door, and when I got there I ran straight up to Grandma's room.

"Grandma, I'm sorry," I said. "You were right. Beryl is real. I heard her. She has Vanessa!"

But was that right? It sounded like Vanessa was being held hostage. What about her aunt Tilda? Had Beryl taken her, too?

"We have to help her!" I continued, because Grandma Jeannie wasn't answering. She was breathing hard, and even though it was cool in her room, sweat dripped down her forehead.

Mom came in then. She must have heard me run in, or else she heard me yelling.

"Josie, calm down," she said, trying to sound soothing. She stepped in and put a hand on my shoulder.

"No! You don't understand. Vanessa is hurt and we need to help her. Beryl has her!"

Mom sighed. She didn't answer at first. When I looked at her, she looked almost as tired as Grandma Jeannie.

"Josie, enough."

"What?"

Mom looked from Grandma to me. Then she knelt down so she was eye level and lowered her voice to a whisper.

"It's bad enough that your grandmother believes

these things," she said. "But I'd hoped that you were old enough to understand the difference between fantasy and reality. Beryl isn't real. There isn't any danger."

"But—"

"No, Josie. I don't want to hear any more of this. Your grandmother is sick. You know that. And this is only going to make it worse. Come on."

She stood and began walking away, leading me out with her.

"But Vanessa—"

"Is fine. I just called her house."

That made me stop in my tracks.

"You called her? How?"

"She left her number with me last night. So we could arrange another sleepover with her aunt. She also wanted to apologize for leaving so rudely earlier."

"You spoke with Vanessa?" I asked. I couldn't believe it.

"No," Mom said. "I spoke with her aunt, just after you ran off. I figured you might go there."

My heart was hammering. This didn't make any sense. Vanessa and her aunt were trapped with the monster. Did that mean . . . maybe Beryl was forcing her aunt to talk on the phone? Like robbers did to their hostages, to make the police think everything was okay.

Why was I the only one who knew that everything *wasn't* okay?

"You spoke to her aunt?"

"Yes, Josie. And she and Vanessa are both just fine."

"They are?"

"Yes, Josie."

She sighed again. We were headed downstairs, toward the kitchen.

"You see?" she said. "You're just letting your imagination get the better of you. Everything's going to be fine. In fact, her aunt Tilda and I made plans for you. Next Friday, you're going to stay over at their place. Tilda said she would be very excited to have you stay with her."

Even though she said it cheerily, it still made my skin go cold.

There was no way I would stay the night there. Not with Beryl hiding out.

It didn't make me feel any better to know that Vanessa's aunt had talked to my mom. In fact, it made me feel worse. This meant that no one would believe me.

I only knew one thing: Beryl *was* real. And she had my best friend and her aunt trapped.

It was up to me to save them.

33

"Hello?"

Vanessa's voice on the other end of the phone made me sigh with relief.

It was after dinner, and I'd known I wouldn't be able to sleep if I didn't at least call Vanessa to see if she was okay. I'd thought about calling the cops but I knew they wouldn't believe me. This was my only hope.

"Vanessa?" I asked. "Are you . . . are you okay?"

"Yeah," she replied. "I'm sorry about running off earlier. I don't know what got into me. I think I was just worried about making your grandma more sick, you know?"

She sounded just like her normal self, and that made me suspicious.

"Are you sure you're feeling okay?" I asked. "I mean . . ." How could I say this? If there was a monster in the house, if she was being held hostage, would Beryl be listening in? "Are you alone?"

"What? Yeah, I'm okay. And no, I'm not alone. My aunt's here. Are you sure *you're* okay?"

My heart started hammering. Was she trying to speak in code? Did she mean someone else was there besides her aunt?

"Josie?" she asked. I realized I hadn't answered.

"I'm fine," I lied. "I just . . . you, um, left your bag here."

"I know," she said. "Could you bring it tomorrow?"

"You'll be at school?"

"Of course I will, silly. Why wouldn't I be?"

Because you were crying a few hours ago. Because it sounded like you were trapped.

I wanted to ask her who she'd been talking to. But I also didn't want to risk that person listening in. If

Beryl was in the house, I had to believe that she was watching.

"I don't know," I said. Ugh, I wished I could just ask her what I really wanted to. "I guess . . . okay, never mind. I guess I'll just see you at school."

"Are you sure you're okay?" Vanessa asked.

"Yeah. Just . . . weird day. Grandma's not feeling too well."

"Oh, I'm sorry to hear that," Vanessa said. She honestly did sound like she meant it. "I hope she gets better soon."

"Me too," I replied.

I was surprised by the urgency in my voice.

I sounded like my life depended on it.

34

"Josie?" Anna asked.

It was late. Probably around midnight, and we had school tomorrow. I'd spent the rest of the day doing homework and trying to distract myself.

I wasn't surprised to hear from her when she padded into my room.

"Yes, Anna?"

"I can't sleep."

I wasn't surprised, because I couldn't sleep either. Even with my window closed, I could hear the noises outside. More than just night animals—more than owls hooting or stray dogs barking.

I could hear Beryl.

The rasp of her voice in the wind. The scratch of her words in the tree branches. The tap of her clawed fingers every time a branch struck my window. It had gotten so much worse over the weekend.

Even though I was curled up in bed, and even though the stale air in here was hot, I was shivering.

I didn't even tell Anna to come in. She ran toward my bed the moment I pulled back the covers.

"She's out there," Anna whispered. She snuggled closer to me.

"I know," I said. "But she can't get in here."

Only . . . in the middle of the night something happened.

I'd fallen asleep. I started to dream of a long, dark hallway, of Vanessa holding my hand, telling me to follow. Of Beryl, waiting at the end of the hall. Calling out. Calling out to me.

No.

Calling out to Anna.

Anna.

"Anna?" I whispered, rolling over.

She was curled up in bed, and even though I know

she didn't have it with her when she came in, the doll was clutched tight in her hands. It seemed to be laughing at me.

Or maybe it wasn't the doll. I could hear something outside. Not something. Some*one*. Beryl. Laughing. And calling Anna's name.

I reached for the doll. She shouldn't have it in here. It wasn't safe. If Mom came in. Or Grandma . . .

The moment my fingers touched the doll, Anna opened her eyes, and I bit back a scream.

"I'm so hot," she said, her voice distant. "I need fresh air."

Outside, the laughing grew louder, and I swore I heard Beryl calling to Anna. Just like in the dream. Except now, she sounded victorious.

"Anna, don't—"

But she was already out of the bed and walking toward the window, like she was sleepwalking, the doll still held tight to her chest.

I stumbled out of bed. The sheets tangled around my feet and tripped me, and when I managed to stand Anna was already at the window. One hand on the windowsill.

"Anna!" I called.

She started lifting the window. The moment she did, a terrible howling sound spilled through the crack. Like wind. Like manic laughter.

And through it all, I heard Beryl calling—"*come to me, come to meeeee.*"

I ran toward Anna and tried to slam the window shut, but she blocked my way. She had the doll held to her chest like a baby. Its head peeked over her shoulder. And it was laughing at me.

The doll. It shouldn't be here. The doll was doing this to her!

I grabbed for it. Tried to tug it from Anna's hands. But the moment I touched it, I flinched back with a yelp. The doll was burning hot.

Outside, Beryl's cackles grew louder.

"So hot," Anna whispered.

She began climbing through the window.

Outside, through the wind and the laughter, I saw a shadow at the edge of the yard. Watching. Beckoning.

Panic raced through my chest. I tried to hold Anna back but she was strong. Too strong. *Unnaturally* strong. She got one leg up.

If I didn't act fast, I'd lose her forever.

I grabbed a blanket that had tangled on the floor and wrapped it around my hand. Then I grabbed the doll and yanked it from her grasp, throwing it at the wall behind us.

Anna screamed.

And then, a second later, she collapsed to the floor.

"Anna, Anna!"

The laughter outside turned to an angry howl. I tugged the window shut, barely blocking out the noise, and knelt beside my sister.

"Anna!" I yelled.

She blinked.

"What?" she asked groggily.

"Anna—"

She looked around. "What happened? Why am I on the floor?"

"You don't remember?"

She shook her head. Then, mumbling to herself, she picked herself up and walked to the bed. When she collapsed atop it, she was asleep immediately.

I sat there for a moment, watching her sleep, my heart pounding so loud I couldn't hear anything else.

Like the laughter outside.

I stood and looked out the window, but there was no shadow. No Beryl waiting by the woods.

When I turned back, however, the doll was still there. Standing on its own by the wall. Watching me.

It was still smiling, as if to say, *Next time*.

I grabbed it and shoved it into an empty shoebox. I'd throw it out tomorrow, when it was safe to open the window.

If it would ever be safe again.

35

Vanessa had said the doll would rid us of nightmares.

She was wrong.

They hadn't gone away.

They'd built up strength.

I was back in the woods. I wasn't alone in this nightmare. Anna was with me.

We were running, and I wasn't the only one with a partner—Beryl had brought her dolls.

All around us I could hear them running. Scratching. Scurrying. Climbing.

Their tiny porcelain limbs scrambling over tree branches, tiny and not-so-tiny shadows flitting in the moonlight like bats. Glowing shapes leaping between trees like skeletal squirrels. Chittering and laughing. Watching us run and knowing that we were already trapped.

But that just made us run faster.

Our bare feet trampled over stones and twigs and tiny doll bodies. My feet hurt. My chest hurt from breathing so hard and my fingers cramped from holding Anna's hand. I couldn't let her go. I was practically dragging her now, and she was crying, but she didn't stop running. We both knew what would happen if she did. I wouldn't let that happen.

"Look out!" Anna yelled.

She pulled me to a stop. Ahead of us, the path was overrun with little dolls. They scurried toward us like albino spiders, some whole, but most of them broken or mangled.

I screamed.

Then I turned and darted through the woods. There was no path here, and the tree branches stooped low, burdened with tiny doll bodies. They yanked at our hair, giggled as their tiny porcelain fingers scratched my scalp. Others scuttled around our feet, trying to trip us, trying to tug at our heels. They pulled at Anna. Tried to drag her away from me. I clutched tighter. I couldn't let her go. Couldn't let them take her.

We ran through the dark woods, stumbling as we went, the dolls around us laughing and laughing.

Then we reached Vanessa's house.

It appeared suddenly—one moment we were surrounded by trees, the next, we were in her front yard. Only now all the dolls that had been here before were missing. Of course they were; now they were chasing us.

I ran toward the house.

We threw open the front door and thudded inside, but we didn't stop. We ran down the hall, past the empty rooms void of dolls, past bedrooms and empty playrooms. Until we rushed into a room I'd seen before. The one with the door covered in locks.

This one was empty except for a desk with a big glass case on it. And in this case was a necklace—

The necklace Vanessa was always wearing.

I was so captivated that I didn't even lock the door behind us. Anna was by my side, staring at the case.

Then the door swung open.

A terrifying figure hunched in the doorway. She was covered in layers of robes and animal fur, her hair tangled in long waves around her head like dried seaweed. I expected her to have horns or hooves, but she was definitely human, even if her wrinkled skin was the color of old paper and her eyes glowed white as the moon outside.

"*Josie*," she rasped. Her voice. That familiar voice. I'd know it anywhere. "And you've brought dessert."

"No," I said. I stood in front of Anna. "You won't hurt her."

"Hurt her?" Beryl laughed. "I don't want to hurt her. I want to preserve her. Forever." She smiled. "Yes, dear. It will look beautiful on you."

I didn't have time to ask what she meant.

Behind me, I heard a gasp.

When I turned around, Anna stood there, the necklace around her neck and her face frozen in shock.

Only she wasn't Anna anymore.

She was a doll.

36

I woke frantically, a scream lodged in my throat. I was covered in sweat even though Anna had curled all the covers around herself.

She moaned in her sleep, like she was in pain. But at least she was okay. At least she wasn't a doll.

I leaned over to wake her, to ask if she'd had similar dreams.

When I looked at the dresser, I wanted to scream.

Her doll was there. Sitting on my alarm clock, smiling at us. I swore its eyes were glowing.

I didn't think. I grabbed the doll and jumped out of bed, then ran to the window. It was daylight out, and there were no shadows at the edge of the trees. I opened up the window and threw the doll outside. It plummeted to the ground and shattered on the sidewalk, breaking into a million pieces and scattering like snow. My breath heaved and tears were in my eyes. But I'd done it. With the doll gone, we were safe. Safer.

Then I heard an all-too familiar voice on the breeze.

Beryl.

She was close.

And she was laughing.

37

Even though it was light out, it was still too early to be awake. I sat on the floor by the bed, curled up in a blanket, watching the closed windows. And waiting.

Waiting for Beryl to claw her way to us, waiting for my nightmare to become reality and dolls to swarm in. Waiting, and wondering what was going on, wondering if Vanessa was okay. If any of us would be okay.

By the time my alarm went off, I thought I was going to go mad.

Anna woke up when the alarm rang. I turned to

her and was going to ask if she'd had any dreams, but before I had the chance, she leaped out of bed and ran from the room.

She refused to talk to me the rest of the morning, and I had no idea why. Was it about the doll? About waking up in the middle of the night? Did she even remember? If it was, why wouldn't she say so? There were plenty of moments when Mom wasn't around. But she avoided me completely.

It made me confused and sad, but I had other things to worry about now that we'd made it through the night and school was approaching.

Like what I was going to say to Vanessa.

And where the doll I had thrown out the window had gone. When I looked outside at breakfast, there was no porcelain dust on the sidewalk, no broken doll parts. The sidewalk was clean. It was like the doll never existed.

What was going on?

Even though Vanessa said she'd see me at school, even though she'd sounded okay on the phone, I didn't quite believe it. I knew in my heart that she was being held captive, that Beryl would never let her go.

Because what was the other option? That I'd made all of that up? The thought scared me more than the events last night had. What if I was becoming like Grandma? What if *I* couldn't tell fantasy from reality anymore?

Which was why, when I saw Vanessa waiting for me outside the school, I felt a rush of relief and dread. Now I would find out the truth.

"Hey," I said when I got close.

"Hey." She held up a bag of cookies. Chocolate chip. "I made these for you. As an apology."

I handed her her overnight bag. She exchanged it for the cookies.

"I shouldn't have run off like that," she said. "I was a bad friend. I hope you'll forgive me."

I looked around. No one was listening in, but that didn't keep me from lowering my voice. "I went to your house."

If I hadn't been watching her so closely, I might not have noticed her eyes going wide, right before she regained composure.

"Why would you do that?"

I didn't want to tell her I was angry with Grandma,

or that I'd been thinking of running away. "I was worried about you."

She looked at her feet.

"I'm okay. But I appreciate how much you care." She paused. "If you came to my house, why didn't you knock?"

I looked around again.

"I heard something," I whispered.

"What?"

"I heard . . . I heard you crying. You were crying, and someone was talking to you. Someone scary. I thought maybe you were being held hostage."

She didn't answer for a while. Kids walked past, talking and laughing and looking at us sideways, but I barely noticed them. It felt like everything in my world rested on her answer.

"There was no one with me last night," she finally said. "Just me and Aunt Tilda." She chuckled and finally looked at me. "Really, Josie, you're letting your imagination get the best of you."

Her smile said it was okay, that she thought it was funny. But I knew the look in her eyes.

She was scared.

38

Vanessa may have shown up to school that day, but after the first class I learned that someone else hadn't.

We were in history, and once more the principal came in.

"Class," she asked, "I'm afraid I am here to ask you, again, if any of you have seen one of your classmates. Charlie Bean did not show up for class today, even though his parents said he left their house. Have any of you heard from him?"

The silence in the room was heavy.

Principal Overton asked a few more questions,

but no one had seen or heard from Charlie today, and Charlie hadn't told anyone he'd be missing class.

"Well," she concluded, looking very sad, "I'm going to be calling your families this afternoon. We will have cops patrolling the school grounds, and until we have more information, all students will be required to get rides to and from school, either from their families or the bus. Don't go anywhere alone, not until we have found Charlie and Karen. And please, report any strangers to an adult. We must watch out for each other right now."

It wasn't until she left that I realized I'd been holding my breath.

Last night, I'd heard Vanessa begging Beryl not to have her bring another. Now I knew what she meant.

Beryl had wanted a child.

And Vanessa had been forced to bring one to her.

39

Vanessa wasn't at lunch when I got there.

I went to our usual table and sat down. In my distraction this morning, I hadn't asked Mom to pack me a lunch, which meant a stale piece of pizza and pudding that was a solid lump. I didn't think I could eat either of them—not just because they were gross, but because my stomach was all knotted up with fear.

I had to confront Vanessa and demand the truth. Either she was being used by Beryl, or she had been lying to me the whole time.

Honestly, I couldn't figure out what was worse. Either my friend was in a lot of trouble, or she had never been my friend at all.

By the time the final lunch bell rang, I realized Vanessa wasn't coming. I left without eating. It felt like I was sleepwalking; I heard the people around me, but I couldn't understand what they were saying, and even though I was moving, it felt like I wasn't going anywhere. I knew that Vanessa wasn't going to be in class when I got there, but it didn't make it any less of a shock to learn I was right.

I didn't see her anywhere, and that just meant I had a lot of time to question and think. Not that my brain was working properly. I couldn't put the pieces together—not in a way that made sense. I still had no idea who or what Beryl was, or how she was involved with Vanessa and her aunt. I didn't know what was happening to the missing kids.

I didn't know why Beryl was apparently coming for me, or why she hadn't gotten me yet.

The rest of the day went by in a blur.

Only one thing stood out, and that was the note that had been taped to the front of my locker.

THIS IS UR FAULT

It didn't help that, for some reason, I felt it was true.

I tore it down and left it crumpled on the ground.

As expected, Vanessa wasn't waiting for me outside the school.

Mom was.

She stood by the flagpole and waved when I came out. I walked over, still dazed.

"Hi?" I asked.

"Hey, honey," she said. "How was your day?"

"Okay."

I wasn't going to tell her the truth: Vanessa had run off and the monsters were real and Grandma had been right all along. I glanced around. The parking lot was filled with parents and guardians picking up their kids, and the line for buses seemed longer than usual. It was crowded. But I didn't see Vanessa. Or my little sister. The realization made my chest constrict.

"Where's Anna?" I asked.

"Already home," Mom said. "I picked her up after

187

lunch because she wasn't feeling well. I don't think she slept much last night."

She looked at me, as if expecting me to explain why. I kept my mouth shut.

"Where's Vanessa?" she asked when we reached the car.

"Went home," I said. It wasn't a lie, but it also wasn't the full truth.

"Are you okay, honey?" she asked.

I nodded.

"Just tired."

"You girls. I don't know why you keep each other up all night."

I wasn't about to tell her that it wasn't either of us—it was the monster in the woods. That last night Anna was almost taken, that we needed to bolt the windows shut to be safe. She already thought I couldn't tell fantasy from reality. I didn't need to make her think so even more.

I just had to be more vigilant from now on. Until Grandma was better. Until she could keep us safe again.

Mom told me to be quiet when I got home. Anna

and Grandma were sleeping, which meant I was left to do my homework on my own.

I considered calling Vanessa, but I knew that I wouldn't get any answers that way. I felt trapped.

So I did my homework up in my room. Or at least I tried to do my homework. I couldn't concentrate on anything. Beryl was taking children and Vanessa might be helping her, and no one believed me. No one except Grandma, and no one believed her.

Still . . .

I left my homework on the floor and went in to talk to Grandma.

I couldn't tell if she was awake, but I couldn't wait around any longer. The room smelled even more like sickness, and Grandma's breathing was heavy.

I sat down on a chair beside her bed and reached out to hold her hand.

"Grandma?" I asked.

She muttered something. I said her name again. She opened her eyes and turned to me.

"Oh, Josie, it's you. I was having such a terrible dream."

"We all have been," I said. Actually, I didn't know

if that was true—had Mom been having nightmares, or just us kids and Grandma?

"I'm so sorry," Grandma said.

"Why?"

"Because I'm too tired to keep you safe."

I sighed. My heart started pounding again.

"That's why I'm here," I said. "I wanted to talk to you. About Beryl."

That made Grandma go from dazed to alert. She pushed herself up in bed. Thankfully, though, she didn't go into one of her episodes. Her eyes were perfectly clear when she looked at me.

"What about Beryl?"

"What is she?" I asked. "How do you know about her? And why is she after us?"

Now it was Grandma's turn to sigh.

"Beryl used to be my friend," Grandma replied sadly. "All those years ago. She and I and our friend Victoria were very close. We did everything together. But Beryl was always a little different. We knew the rumors—people thought Beryl's mom was a witch. And so they thought Beryl was one, too. Little did we know, everyone was right.

"It started with little things. Beryl would turn kids against each other on the playground. And then, when she got older, she got meaner. She loved dolls. And she was always jealous of our friend Victoria, because Victoria's family was very rich and bought her everything she wanted. She had an amazing doll collection. Beryl wanted them for herself.

"One night, we were having a sleepover at Victoria's. Beryl asked to keep one of the dolls, but it was Victoria's favorite, and she wouldn't give it up. So Beryl put a spell on her, and turned her into a doll."

She closed her eyes and took a deep, labored breath. It was like she hadn't told this to anyone else before. And I couldn't blame her—no one else would believe her.

But I . . . I did.

"I tried to get her to turn Victoria back, but Beryl refused. So I left, and I vowed to keep the town safe from Beryl's evil magic. It took many years, and Beryl took many young children and turned them into dolls before I was powerful enough to stop her. But eventually I did, and she has been locked within the woods and her home ever since.

"At least . . . until now. As I grow weak, she grows stronger."

I had to ask, "Is that why she's after us? Is that why you sent Mom to another school?"

Grandma Jeannie nodded sadly, tears streaming down her face.

"I tried to protect you. I told your mother not to bring you two here, but she wouldn't listen. I hoped my rules were enough to keep you safe."

"It's okay, Grandma. We're still safe."

"For now," Grandma said. "But I can't keep you safe forever."

I took her hand. I wanted to comfort her, but I also wanted someone to comfort *me*.

"We'll stay out of trouble," I promised. "We know the rules."

"That won't be enough. She'll find you. She always finds you."

"Then how do we stop her?"

Grandma looked at me long and hard.

"Beryl keeps her magic close. If you can find the key to it, you can stop her. My magic wasn't enough to keep you safe. I charmed this house to protect everyone from her clutches. It wasn't enough, and I spent years practicing. I fear . . . I fear there is nothing you can do."

She started to moan, and I wanted to tell her it would be okay. But I knew that none of this would be okay.

Something wasn't clicking, though. What did Vanessa have to do with any of this? Had Beryl trapped her to do the witch's dirty work? I had to act fast, before Grandma slipped away from me.

"Grandma, my friend Vanessa—why did you yell at her?"

"Because she isn't Vanessa," Grandma told me. Then she started muttering to herself, and I worried that I'd lost her.

Until I heard what she was saying:

"How is she back? How is she back? How is Victoria back?"

46

I couldn't believe what I was hearing. No, I didn't *want* to believe what I was hearing.

Vanessa was actually Victoria? But how? Vanessa was *my* age. And if what Grandma said was true, Victoria was now a doll. A very old doll.

There wasn't a chance to ask any more, though— I knew if I stayed any longer, Grandma Jeannie would only get worse.

"Get some rest, Grandma," I said. "I'll take care of this."

The only problem was, I had no idea *how*.

I headed back to my room. I needed to formulate a plan. Some way to defeat Beryl and keep everyone safe. I needed a miracle.

By dinnertime, the miracle hadn't come.

I'd spent what felt like *hours* writing out ideas, but without the internet or good books on witches nearby, I didn't really have much to go on. I knew from movies that evil spirits hated salt. I also knew they preferred the nighttime, usually midnight. I didn't know much about witches. Especially not ones who turned little kids into dolls. I mean, there were the witches in all the old stories—*The Wizard of Oz*, "Snow White," "Hansel and Gretel"— but I didn't have magic slippers and, even though Vanessa always had baked goods, I didn't think Beryl would fit in the house's tiny oven. I also didn't think I could bring myself to hurt anyone, let alone cook them.

When Mom called up to me that it was time for dinner, I realized I'd only been at work for less than an hour. I rubbed my eyes. My head already hurt from thinking so much. And I still hadn't come up with any ideas. All I knew was, Beryl came out at night—and that meant tonight, we would be at the greatest risk.

I walked past Anna's room when I went to dinner, pressed my ear against her door. I didn't hear anything in there, but that didn't mean much. She might still be asleep. I hoped she was feeling better—if her dreams were anything like mine last night, I could imagine she hadn't slept much.

And, now that I knew there was dark magic at work, I felt bad about blaming the doll on her.

Had it been a spy for Beryl? Was it another little girl locked in a doll's body?

"Anna?" I whispered.

I felt I should apologize to her before dinner. I should try and show her that I was sorry by offering to bring her food or something. I had to protect her, and that meant she had to trust me again.

She didn't respond.

"Anna?" I asked again, a little louder this time.

Mom called from downstairs, "Josie! Dinner!" but I barely heard her. I was listening intently to Anna's door. It was quiet. So quiet.

I turned the handle and stepped inside.

The curtains were drawn and the covers pulled up in a huddle. I crept in. Her room smelled *exactly* like Grandma's, and that had me worried.

"Anna?" I asked again. "How are you feeling? Do you need me to bring anything?"

I stepped closer, letting the door click shut behind me. My heart pounded in my throat.

Still, she didn't answer.

"Anna?"

I reached her bed.

Reached out my hand.

Pulled back the cover.

The doll stared back. *The* doll, the one that Vanessa had given her. The one I'd destroyed. Now its pieces were back together, with all the cracks showing. And it stared at me like it knew I was the one who'd brought it to harm.

How had it gotten back together? How had it gotten back inside?

On the doll was a folded note.

I grabbed the note and unfolded it with shaking hands.

Clara says you are mean.

Clara says I should run away.

So I am.

Good-bye forever.

—Anna

    I remembered what Vanessa had said, about Anna needing to wait to find a friend. I thought about how we'd never met Clara, and how Clara didn't have any parents.

    Clara was working for Beryl, too.

    And she had stolen my sister.

41

Dinner smelled amazing, but I barely paid it any attention as I raced down the steps and out the back door.

Anna's note was crumpled in my pocket, and Mom's voice called out from behind me, but all I could focus on was the woods. The woods, and the witch who had stolen Anna away.

Mom might have followed me. I wasn't sure. I crashed through the trees and the twigs, stumbling and getting scratched, and it reminded me so much of my dream last night. Except there weren't any dolls chasing me today. I was chasing the dolls.

Time seemed to stretch and snap; it felt like I had been running for hours, but I knew that couldn't be the case. Still, that didn't explain why it got darker with every footstep, and why—in seemingly no time at all—the air around me was cold and windy, and the night sky heavy and clear and filled with a wicked moon.

Magic. It had to be.

It also had to be a sort of magic that propelled me forward, a magic that led me to the edge of the glade where Vanessa's house rested. That magic cut out the moment my foot landed on the first broken concrete slab of her sidewalk.

I stopped there, panting heavily, staring out at the house. Lights glowed inside and the moon hovered low overhead, but everything else was dark, dark shadow.

I could hear my mother calling my name. But it was too late. I knew the same magic that drew me in would prevent her from finding me here.

The yard was still overgrown like a nightmare, but the mannequins and the dolls were all gone. That made the hair on my neck stand on end.

If the dolls weren't there, where were they?

I had a feeling I already knew.

It was then that I realized how stupid this was. It was late—or it seemed late—and I was here alone, facing off against an evil monster-witch with an army of dolls at her disposal. And all I had on my side was me. Just little old me, with no magic and no clue how to save Anna. Or myself.

I should have brought my mom. I should have brought Grandma. I should have called the police.

But I hadn't, and here I was, a terrible path before me and no turning back.

I clenched my fists.

I wasn't going to run away from this. I was going to get my sister back, and I was going to put an end to Beryl once and for all. For me. For Anna. For Grandma Jeannie.

Slowly, I crept up to the front door, hoping that maybe they weren't expecting me. Hoping I could surprise them—though I didn't know what I would do if I did. The door was open a crack, and the moment I neared, I heard a familiar voice.

"*Josieee. You've returrrrned.*"

I clenched my teeth and pressed my hand to the door.

It was time to meet the monster.

42

Vanessa's house smelled like baking again.

That was my first realization.

My second was that everything in here had changed. At least, the dolls had.

Before they'd all been looking at the wall. Now they were all turned toward me.

Just like in the dream, their eyes were crossed out and their mouths were open in silent screams. Or near-silent screams. Wind whistled through the door, and it sounded like wailing ghosts.

A shadow shifted at the end of the hall, and I had my first true sighting of Beryl.

I could tell she'd been a woman once. She was hulking and huge, filling up the whole hallway with her shadowy body. Her skin was wrinkled and pale as moonlight, her eyes white pits. Two clawed hands reached from the folds of her shadowy dress, her nails long and vicious.

When she smiled, her teeth were all pointed like a wolf's.

I held back a scream. Even though I wanted to scream. Very, very badly.

"Josieee," she rasped. Her smile widened.

"Where is my sister?" I yelled. I tried to keep my voice from shaking, but it didn't work.

"She is here. Home. Your home."

With one gnarled finger, she gestured to the door beside me.

I gulped and walked over.

Inside, on the sofa, were two life-size dolls. One was Vanessa. The other was . . .

"Anna!" I yelled.

I ran into the room and knelt by her side.

There was nothing I could do, though: her skin was porcelain and her eyes were glazed marbles. Her lips were painted in a smile, but I could tell from her eyes that she was shocked.

"What did you do to her?" I demanded. Tears welled up in my eyes.

"I brought her home," Beryl replied. "So she can be mine. Forever."

"She's not yours," I said. "She's my sister. She's not yours!"

"She came to me," Beryl rasped. "She is mine now. Just like the other children are mine now. And there is nothing you can do to save her!"

No, no, there had to be a way to save them. I might not have magic, but I had my brain. I looked from Anna to Vanessa. Vanessa's doll wasn't wearing her necklace.

The necklace!

I jumped to my feet and picked up the Anna doll—she was remarkably light—and ran out of the room.

Beryl howled in anger behind me.

"Nooo!" she wailed. "Bring her back!"

I had to hope my dreams had been right. That I would find where I needed to go. That the necklace actually had a power.

I darted down the hall while Beryl chased after me, snarling like the beast she'd become. I didn't look back—I knew that if I did, she'd catch me, and I'd never escape or save anyone.

There!

I pushed open the door and then slammed it shut behind me. There was an old-fashioned dead bolt on it, and I locked the door just in time. Beryl thudded against it and howled again.

"Come out of there!" she yelled.

But we'd made it. I leaned Anna against the table and looked at my prize: Vanessa's necklace. It seemed to shine with its own light from where it rested in its glass case. I could almost feel the magic radiating from it. I knew this was what I needed to do.

With trembling hands, I pulled the necklace from the box and draped it over Anna's neck.

There was a gust of wind and a whirl of lights, and I watched transfixed as Anna's body slowly turned from doll to girl.

"Josie!" she gasped when the magic was complete. She fell into my arms and hugged me.

"Anna, you're okay!"

But our relief was short-lived. Beryl pounded on the door, making books fall off the shelves. We didn't have much time before she broke in.

"I have to save the others," I said, reaching for the necklace around Anna's neck.

"No!" she said. "If you take it off, I turn back into a doll."

"What?" I felt the world falling down around me. If she couldn't take it off, I couldn't save anyone else.

"Yeah. But I think there's a way," she said.

The door shuddered again. We had to hurry!

Anna went on. "I heard Beryl. The necklace holds the spell—the only way to break it is to make Beryl wear it."

"But then I have to leave you as a doll!"

"It's the only way," she said. She took my hands and put them on the necklace. "Do it. I'll be fine. It doesn't hurt."

"I'm so sorry I didn't believe you," I said, tears in my eyes.

"It's okay. You believe me now. You'll save me, I know it."

Crying, I lifted the necklace off her neck.

A moment later, she was a doll again.

I clutched the necklace tightly and turned to the door.

Then I stepped forward and put my hand on the lock.

It was time to end this, once and for all.

43

I turned the lock and opened the door.

Beryl floated outside, her robes fluttering around her like wings. When she saw that I held the necklace, she snarled and reared back.

"What do you think you're doing?" she growled.

"I'm ending this," I replied.

That made her laugh.

"You have no power here. You can't save them. You are alone. As you will always be alone."

Her words cut through me.

I'd felt alone this whole time. Ever since I moved here. Only one person had made me not feel that way.

"What did you do to Vanessa?" I asked. "Why has she been helping you?"

"You mean Victoria? She has no choice. Just as you will have no choice. She is my servant. As you will be. It will be my greatest revenge, for all your grandmother has done to me."

She stepped forward, but I reached my hand up with the necklace, and she flinched back.

"I know your secret. This is how you control them. But if you wear it, your magic breaks. They'll be free."

I expected her to howl in fear. Instead, she started laughing.

"Perhapssss. But if you destroy my powers, every doll will return to their real age. And your dear friend 'Vanessa' will be an old woman. If she even lives. But if you join me, you can be her friend forever. Otherwise, you'll stay lonely until the end of time."

That made me pause.

Saving everyone might mean Vanessa became an old woman. Or it could kill her. Could I do that?

Then I remembered hearing her crying the other day, when I'd snuck up to the house, and I realized that yes—she would want to be free, no matter the cost. She'd want everyone else to be free as well.

I also knew that I would never get close enough to Beryl to put the necklace on her. I had to lure her in.

Sighing, I bowed my head.

"You're right. I can't do it. I don't want to be alone anymore."

Beryl laughed.

"Don't worry, Josie. This will only hurt a bit."

She reached out and grabbed my shoulder.

Reached for the necklace.

And then, before she could take it from me, I sprung into action and looped the chain around her neck.

She screamed the moment it touched her skin.

The whole house shook and wind burst through the windows, whipping curtains and knocking over lamps. Lights flashed and shadows swirled, and I stepped back in horror as Beryl whirled and screamed like a tornado, collapsing in on herself.

Only moments later, she was nothing more than a pile of black dust and a necklace covered in soot.

"Josie?" Anna whispered from behind me.

A girl. Not a doll.

"Anna!" I yelled. I turned and gave her a huge hug.

"Is it over?" she asked.

"It's over," I replied, squeezing her tight. "Everything's going to be fine now."

"Josie?" came another voice. Weaker. Older. But I still recognized it.

Vanessa.

I took Anna's hand and ran into the living room.

Vanessa was there, on the sofa. And in the space of moments, she had aged. She was wrinkled, and her hair was gray.

"Vanessa!" I ran over and knelt at her side, taking her hand. As always, her skin was cold. She looked so old, but when she looked at me, her eyes were just as youthful as before.

"You did it," she said. She squeezed my hand, but her grip was weak. "You saved us. Thank you."

"But I couldn't save you, not really."

Tears were beginning to form.

"It's okay, Josie. I've been under Beryl's command for far too long, and have done terrible things. I'm sorry I could never tell you the truth—her magic prevented it. I can finally rest now."

She took a deep, rattling sigh.

"I'm just glad Beryl's evil has ended." When she looked at me and smiled, her eyes filled with tears. "And that after all these years, I knew what friendship felt like again. Tell Jeannie good-bye for me, will you?"

I nodded.

And, with another sigh, she closed her eyes.

If I pretended, it almost looked like she was sleeping.

Meanwhile, in the hall, there was the sound of voices. Of running and shouting, tears and laughter. I heard footsteps racing down the hall, but I didn't go to see them. Anna stood by my side, holding my hand, as we watched my friend slowly vanish into a cloud of dust and stars. By the time we got into the hall, all the other children had disappeared.

Like us, they didn't want to stay here any longer than they had to.

44

Local children who had been missing for days or years had found their way home. I watched it on the news, saw their tear-filled reunions with family and friends. It made me feel a little better, to know I'd helped so many people. But I was still sad over losing Vanessa.

Anna and I had walked home hand in hand after that terrible night. She hadn't needed to sleep in my bed again. Both of us stopped having nightmares.

Grandma Jeannie was feeling better. Lots better. She'd started having sun tea on the back porch with us again, and she didn't seem to look at the woods with as much fear. Together, she and Anna and I had buried the magical locket and Vanessa's doll in our backyard. Grandma even did a little spell over the burial site to keep it hidden and safe.

Anna asked me over and over if Clara's name had appeared on the news. But it never did. Maybe, like Vanessa, she'd been given a different name. Or maybe not. There was no way for us to know.

Going back to school was hard. Without Vanessa, everything seemed a little off. At least no one was leaving scary notes on my locker. It made me wonder . . . had everyone known about Vanessa and her tie to Beryl? Maybe my grandmother hadn't been the only one warning kids away from the woods. Maybe everyone else had just been trying to keep me—the new girl who didn't know better—safe from a threat.

Slowly, I started to make some new friends. Karen and Charlie, the kids who had been recently turned into dolls, started hanging out with me at lunchtime. We never spoke about what happened. We didn't need to.

Honestly? I thought everything had gone back to normal.

Or at least as normal as things could be out here, anyway.

I even began leaving my window open at night to let the cool breeze in. There weren't any whispers or monsters calling my name.

It was nice to feel like a normal kid again. Not worrying about magic or dolls or witches.

Things were finally going to be okay.

45

It was a little less than two weeks after I defeated Beryl.

"Josie!" Mom called out. "Time for breakfast!"

I curled the sheets tighter around me. Monday. I didn't want to go to school. We had a quiz in science today. Maybe five more minutes of sleep . . .

BEEP BEEP BEEP!

My alarm clock started blaring.

I reached over to turn it off.

My hand bumped into something.

Slowly, I opened my eyes, tried to make my vision adjust. I couldn't believe what I saw.

There was a doll on my nightstand.

A doll that looked an awful lot like Beryl.

About the Author

K. R. Alexander scours the world for fantastic and true stories (but this book is made up . . . right?) and is an avid collector of things mysterious and macabre. K. R. is the author of many books for adults and teens, though they write under various guises.

K.R. recommends having your toys face the wall at night.

Just in case.